WITHOUT YOU

BY PAULA WILKES

On waking I stretch and instinctively reach my arm out to caress your back. For that split second I forget that you are no longer there and wonder if she rubs your back to wake you up. Hot tears start to fill my eyes but I will not let them fall. I promised myself on the day that you left that I would not cry, a shiver runs through my body as my mind shoots back to that awful day when you told me.

We had only just come back from a lovely holiday down in Cornwall, where we had walked holding hands along leafy lanes, long beach walks over golden sand and had enjoyed long lazy lunches in quaint old pubs.

'I don't know why this is a shock to you!' Steve had angrily thrown at me 'you must have realised that we have nothing in common, anymore!'

'But all week you've been telling me how much you love me' came my tearful reply.

'I do love you but I'm not in love with you." A stab in the heart would have been easier to take 'I'm moving out, now don't start crying the sooner I go the easier it will be. I'll make sure that you have everything you need, so you needn't worry about money'

After a few days I mustered up the courage to go and see a solicitor that I had found in the yellow pages. I knew instinctively that Steve would use the company solicitor who was a golfing buddy of his.

I didn't contest the divorce, there seemed no point, if he didn't want me I might as well let him go with dignity. The divorce went through very quickly and to my surprise and Steve's horror I received more than expected. In a strange way it was my revenge watching the colour drain from his face when the judge announced the amount of the settlement. I could tell that he was trying desperately to contain the growing rage that was building up inside him.

His solicitor had argued that the company had been based purely on Steve's hard work. This was an absolute lie as I had been very involved within the company from the start, sending out invoices and even delivering items to customers when the drivers were too busy or on holiday.

Steve and his clever solicitor had overlooked one very important fact, the company accountant, at the start of the business had advised that I should be named as a co-director something to do with tax, I had just signed the paper put in front of me and hadn't given it another thought. However, this was still in force which meant that I owned half of the company. So if he wanted me out of his life completely he had to buy me out.

After a great deal of huffing and puffing a settlement was reached and I walked away with a very considerable sum, plus the family home.

On leaving the court I caught sight of Steve and his new partner, as they walked across the road to his shiny sleek new jaguar. A thought sprung into my head 'a shiny sleek new jaguar and a shiny sleek new girlfriend' but he didn't look happy, I could see from the way he was waving his arms about, as he always did when he hadn't got his own way, that she was going to see a different side of her 'sugar daddy' that maybe she hadn't seen before.

As he turned to get into the car his eyes met mine, for a second I thought that he was going to say something but he just scowled and got into the car.

She turned following his eye's to look at me, I gave her my most triumphant smile and mouthed "Good luck, you're going to need it" to her. She abruptly turned away but not before I had seen the pensive look on her face.

She actually wasn't what I had expected at all as she looked in her late 30's a little plump with short dark hair. I had imagined some young thing all legs and blond hair, I was glad that I had at last seen her.

Within half an hour of waking, hair still wet from the shower, I am sat at the kitchen table coffee in one hand and my trusty pen in the other ready to make a start on my 'to do' list of what needs to be done today.

I find that I can't concentrate with the rain lashing against the window and I don't know why but everything today seems very hum drum and boring.

Glancing around the kitchen for inspiration, my eyes come to rest on the colourful postcard that my dear friend Suzie sent from her home in Barbados, after she emigrated there 20 years ago straight after her parents died. She figured that there was nothing left to keep her in England and she wanted some adventure and more importantly some sun. So one day she closed her eyes and stuck a pin in a world map and the rest is history.

From what she had told me she had become quite an entrepreneur and now had 4 shops dotted around the various islands of the Caribbean, selling top of the range merchandise, shipped in from around the world.

Since the divorce she has constantly nagged me to go and visit and can't understand my reluctance but I don't want to tell her that I'm afraid. Afraid to move forward with my life, but also afraid not to. Since marrying Steve 30 years ago I haven't been anywhere on my own, let alone on an aeroplane to somewhere so distant and so very exotic.

"What are you waiting for?" was her usual comment "come on girl, let's have some fun".

Sitting there all alone in my kitchen with the rain hammering down outside a thought suddenly struck me "Well exactly what am I waiting for" I almost run out into the hall and pick up the phone, my fingers tremble as I dial the number.

"Hello" comes a muffled voice

"Hi Suzie" I try to sound as cheerful as I can "are you okay?"

"Polly, is that you? Are you drunk?" I think I hear a yawn

"Oh dear god what time is it there? Did I wake you? I'm so sorry" everything comes out in a tumble and without waiting for her to respond "I'm coming to see you, well if you don't mind?"

"It's 4.00 am and yes I was asleep, but you can wake me anytime with news like that" she was laughing "what has suddenly brought this on? And when are you arriving?"

"I've just decided that you're right, what the hell am I waiting for" my legs start to shake and I sit down heavily on the stairs next to the telephone table "I need to sort out a couple of things, someone to look after the house, tickets, currency, but I should like to come as soon as possible, if that suits you?"

"To damn right it suits me, get on that plane right now" I could tell from her voice that she was delighted "please don't change your mind. Message me when you have your flight times and I'll meet you at the airport" hesitating she continued "Don't let anything or anyone stop you, this could be the making of you. Now go away and let me sleep, we cougars need our beauty sleep. Love you, see you soon" with that she was gone.

Chapter 2

The flight had taken slightly longer than expected and I was glad when the seatbelt sign flashed on. The couple sitting next to me had bickered for most of the 9 hour flight, mainly due to the man wanting to order alcohol throughout the flight. Luckily I had managed to secure some headphones which allowed me to syphon a lot of the argument out. I was very glad when eventually after yet another whisky he fell asleep. The snoring I could put up with!

I always marvel at why as soon as the seatbelt light goes out people jump to their feet as if their lives depend on getting their hand luggage down from the overhead compartments. I could never understand this urge, it seemed most prevalent in middle aged men, wanting to be first off of the plane. As everyone knows you will, 9 times out of 10, have to wait at the carousel for the luggage so why panic.

Steve had been the same, if I didn't immediately get to my feet you would think that the world was about to end. I would be chastised like a naughty school girl for letting other people off the plane before me.

Thanking the cabin crew I step through the open aircraft door and the heat hits me. Carefully making my way down the steep aeroplane steps I'm very glad that I decided to travel in a maxi dress as the little air that there is, swirls around the hem and I can feel it wafting around my legs.

Grantley Adams International Airport was very busy and I tried to keep up with some of the passengers that I recognised from the flight, who all seemed to know where they were going. By the time we arrived at the correct luggage carousel, to my surprise, it was already crammed with cases. I was very glad that I had chosen a quite, well for me, outrageous case with big pink and purple butterflies on it. I remember the look on the sales assistants face when I chose this one. I'm sure that she thought 'nutty old lady' as this was intended, I think, for younger cliental.

Passing through immigration and customs is always an ordeal for me. Surely I can't be the only one that always feels guilty when walking through the nothing to declare corridor. Never sure whether to make eye contact with the officers who man these areas or not. I always think that a hand is suddenly going to clamp down onto my shoulder and I will be hauled away to answer lots of questions or locked in a secure room, with them mistakenly thinking that I'm a drug smuggler or the like. So with a pounding heart I am very grateful when I walk out into the arrivals area without incident.

Quickly scanning the many smiling faces waiting for loved ones my heart sinks when I realise that Suzie is not there waiting for me. Slowly I walk past all of the other passengers getting hugs or talking to travel guides. What should I do my mobile won't work here and I have no change for the land phones. Looking around a flood of emotion sweeps over me, what the hell am I doing? I feel so lost and, yes, frightened.

My mind races back to two days ago when Steve finally came to the house to collect the rest of his junk from the garage. I wasn't sure whether to tell him about my plans or not.

"I'm going away for a while" I cheerfully said. My heart pounding so hard that I thought it might break through my chest wall.

"Right" he mumbled "you visiting your Mother?" he didn't stop what he was doing, but carried on loading his car, not seeming to be at all bothered or interested.

Nonchalantly I continued "Oh goodness no! I'm off to see Suzie"

"Suzie? Suzie who?" suddenly as if he had received a blow to the head he spluttered "Suzie. Barbados Suzie?"

"I fly out tomorrow" this was said with the gay abandonment as if it was an everyday occurrence "Margaret is coming to house sit. I've told her that I have a year's visa and she's more than happy to stay indefinitely. She loves being here".

"But you can't even find your own way out of Waitrose. How will you manage in Barbados?" as if in shock he sat down heavily on the edge of the boot of his car, he suddenly started to laugh "I don't believe you. No you're having me on"

"Steve dear" I mustered as much sarcasm as I could "why are you bothered? In case you have forgotten I am no longer your responsibility. If I get lost in transit well so what! Now have you finished, is this the last of your stuff?" when he didn't reply I continued "please take everything you need today as I don't want Margaret bothered when I'm away" with this I started to turn towards the house "Oh! And Steve please close your mouth you look like you're catching flies" with a satisfied smile I walked head held high into the house.

"Polly, Polly" spinning around to my great relief there is Suzie hurrying towards me, her dress flying out behind her showing her tanned legs "Oh my god Polly I'm sorry got caught up in traffic" she gives me a great big bear hug and all of my worries suddenly disappear.

Holding me away from her she looks me up and down and gives a low whistle "Well my hot Momma, look at you. You look great. You've lost weight and I must say you look the best that I've seen you in years. I'm going to have trouble keeping the local boys away from you" looking at my startled face she throws her head back and lets out an almighty laugh "Sweet Polly, you are allowed to look hot and sexy. Now come on we have lots to catch up on"

The drive from the airport to the outskirts of Bridgetown was a revelation, the sight of the sugar canes standing tall and proud against the beautiful cloudless sky, looked so majestic. Suzie acted like a tour guide pointing out interesting places and giving me the low down on local customs.

"Now then, what is the first thing that you would like to do" she asks above the music blaring out from the car radio.

"A shower" looking down at my crumpled dress "and something to eat"

"You have just travelled for nearly 9 hours and it's a shower you want" she laughs "but actually that's not a bad idea. Let's get you settled in and then we can walk down to PetePete's restaurant. He makes some of the best Caribbean food you will ever taste"

"PetePete's?" I query

"Yep, his motto is the food is so good he named his restaurant twice" she starts to sing the Frank Sinatra song New York New York, but inserts PetePete's instead of New York New York "believe me he will tell you all about it when you meet him later"

Chapter 3

I let the warm water from the overhead shower wash over me. It feels good after the hours spent sitting on the aeroplane. Lathering soap over my now lean body I can't stop a smile from forming, at least the divorce had one positive effect as I've lost nearly 2 stone without even trying.

As I step out of the shower I catch a glimpse of my naked body in the full length mirror on the opposite side of the bathroom. I twist this way and that to get a good look at myself, as I do I remember Suzie's comment at the airport "Well my hot Momma look at you". Indeed look at me!

After dressing I leave my hair loose letting the warm air dry it naturally. Normally I would blow dry and flat iron to get rid of my natural curls. But now I don't have to worry about looking, as Steve would say, like a mad woman.

Steve always hated it when I allowed my hair to stay curly "For god's sake woman you're not a teenager. I'm not taking you out looking like a mad tinker woman, go and straighten it" dutifully I would do his bidding.

Wandering through Suzie's house I marvel at how colourful everything is, against the drab magnolia of my home in England. Suzie had explained on the journey from the airport that her home had started life as a 'Chattel House' and that the original building was completely made of wood. When she moved in she felt that it was a bit small and had decided to have an extension built on the back of the house with a porch added to the front. Her home now boasted 2 bedrooms with their own private bathroom, the Barbadian workmen had thought this very English.

The lovely open plan kitchen/dining room was beautifully decorated with lots of local artefacts, most of which seemed to be painted in bright reds and greens with splashes of yellow.

The sitting room overlooks the garden which again is full of colour, huge red and yellow flowers stand majestically along the garden fence as if they own that space. Later I learned that these are the national flower 'The Pride of Barbados'. Everything is so very different and exotic against my home.

I find Suzie sitting on the swing seat on the front porch. Her tanned legs spread out in front of her "Oh good, just in time" she says as she holds out a glass to me "this is to welcome you to my home and to a new you" clinking my glass with hers "you look great with your hair like that, I never knew that you had curly hair"

The rum punch hit the spot and sitting next to her on the swing seat in the late afternoon sun I wondered why I hadn't done this before.

"Are you okay with everything?" Suzie looked into her glass as she asked "you know at home!"

I gulped another mouthful of the lovely smooth rum "it still feels strange cooking for one, waking up alone, not having a man about the place….."

Suzie reached across and held my hand "Did he leave you alright for money? Please don't think that I'm being noisy, but you put a lot of work into that company of his, not to mention the hours that you slogged away at the beginning packing all of those machine bits"

I explained about the clever accountant and the fact that as co-director half of the company belonged to me.

"Both Steve and his lawyer looked dumbfounded when the judge made his ruling. I walked away with a very nice settlement. I didn't realise that the company was doing so well and worth so much" at this point I couldn't help but laugh "a few years ago, his solicitor advised Steve to sign over the house to me, don't ask me why. I'm sure it was some tax dodge or the like. He explained to me that it was something to do with not having too many assets in his name"

Suzie looked at me in amazement "so you walked away with the house as well" I nodded and we both hugged each other "Ha, I bet his new fancy woman didn't like that. This really calls for another drink"

"I think that I'd rather have something to eat, if you don't mind?" right on cue my stomach grumbled loudly, which made us both laugh again.

"Right PetePete's it is then"

Chapter 4

We walk down into Bridgetown, with Suzie still acting as a tourist guide pointing out the Parliament Buildings, major banks etc. We walk along Broad Street, which is one of the main duty free shopping areas and there on the corner she points out PetePete's.

From the name I expected PetePete's, or PP as apparently the locals call it, to be a small unassuming café/bar, how wrong was I! The restaurant wraps around the corner from Broad Street and the next road, which I think is Swan Street. The outside has red canopies over every window. These are monogrammed with two large P's depicted in gold which seem to sparkle in the early evening sunshine.

The restaurant would rival any fine London establishment, the brass that adorns the large spotlessly clean heavy glass entrance doors shines in the sunlight and the marble floor looks as though no one has ever walked on it or as my mother would have said "looks like you could eat your dinner off of that, it's so clean".

Walking into the foyer of the restaurant I suddenly wish that I had worn something a little classier. I'm about to say exactly that to Suzie when a very large man with a shaved head and dressed in an immaculate cream linen suit comes hurrying towards us arms outstretched "Well, well, my little chicken has returned to the roost" with that he swoops Suzie up in his arms and starts to carry her through the restaurant, I trot along behind "PP has a very special table for you"

"Pete, for goodness sake put me down, people are looking" Suzie is giggling like a schoolgirl "my friend will wonder what on earth sort of place I've brought her to"

"Oh, chicken they're only looking because their jealous that it's you in my arms and not them "he lets out a laugh which is as deep as his voice. Turning to me, with Suzie still in his arms, he gives a low whistle as he looks me up and down "Are you English? You look more like a Spanish siren" his deep laugh seems to rumble up from his belly as he speaks. Placing Suzie safely back on her feet, he rubs his chin and again slowly looks me up and down "indeed I shall call you Chiquita, my precious little one"

With that he motioned to a waiter who was hovering nearby "Sunny whatever these two lovely ladies want is on the house"

Taking my hand he looks deep into my eyes, I felt my knees go weak and I felt as though butterflies had invaded my stomach "My welcome for a beautiful lady to our beautiful island" with that he kissed my hand before turning and walking out of the restaurant.

"My, oh my" Suzie took a sip of her drink that Sunny had brought to the table "I think that you've made an impression. Never seen him quite so goo-goo"

"Don't be silly. I'm sure that he's that charming to everyone" but as I said it I felt myself blush "now come on Miss Tourism what should I eat?"

Suzie recommended that I try a traditional dish of Chicken, Macaroni Pie and Peas n' Rice. This was indeed one of the most delicious meals that I had eaten in a long time.

After we had finished our meal we wander arm in arm along the seafront towards the main port. I had never seen so many large boats in one place. I especially like the big white Catamaran's that seem, to me, to be holding court over the smaller boats anchored nearby.

We find a nice little bar and settle ourselves at an outside table people watching, whilst sipping our rum punches through long straws. Looking at my friend as she tilts her head up to the late sun, I suddenly feel very free. "I truly understand why you love it here so much. No one seems to expect you to behave in a certain way" I take a long drink from my glass "look at me I would never have gone out to eat like this" I gesture with my free hand to my hair and down over my dress "I would have spent hours blow drying my hair, put on a knee length dress, heels and a full makeup. I've only been here for a few hours and I already feel different"

Suzie places her glass back on the table and takes my hand "my darling girl, that's because you have been living to someone else's beat" patting my hand she continues "you look beautiful" laughing she tugs me to my feet "come on Chiquita let's get you home, I want to show you some of my empire in the morning"

And so for the next 6 months my life settled into a nice little routine of accompanying Suzie on buying trips to the surrounding islands. She had lots of local ladies making the most diverse collection of clothing, from beachwear to the most beautiful gowns that she would pay them very little money for making, but they would be sold in her boutique shops for an absolute fortune.

We would either travel by speed boat or if Pete's small private plane was available we would use that. This always made me feel like some aging rock star. I imagined people trying to guess who had arrived by private plane when we landed at the various airports. But in truth I don't suppose anyone took any notice.

On days that Suzie had private meetings with either her accountant or solicitor I would occupy myself sightseeing or enjoy a lazy day in the garden reading.

But little did I know how quickly things would change.

Chapter 5

A loud noise in the back yard woke me from my sleep, after a while I heard Suzie's voice she sounded very angry "What the hell do you mean no money!" she shouted.

Cautiously I crept out of bed and peeped through the slats of the blind, the scene that confronted me was horrible.

Suzie was holding a young girl by the shoulders and was shaking her very forcefully whilst shouting right in her face "No bloody money, don't give me that, the cruise ships are in and your telling me you made no money" with that she pushed the girl away from her with such force that the young girl was sent flying "I take it that you want to stay in Bridgetown?" Suzie stood over the now obviously frightened girl her voice was almost a growl, the girl said something but from the movement of her head I knew that she had confirmed that she wanted to stay "in that case you had better get your dumbass to work and bring me double tomorrow. Now get out of here" the young girl struggled to her feet and ran out of the garden as fast as she could.

I sank down on the bed what the hell had that been all about. Why would Suzie expect the girl to bring her money and why would she want to take money from her. I knew that when her parents had died they had left her independently wealthy, so the scene that I had just witnessed didn't make any sense. I decided that I wouldn't say anything just yet as the whole incident had left me quite shaken. On hearing Suzie walking down the corridor to my room I quickly got back into bed and pretended to be asleep.

"Hey sleepy head" Suzie gently shook me, not like she had shaken the young girl a moment ago "come on, up you get we have things to do and people to see" as she left the room she called over her shoulder "breakfast in 15 minutes"

Walking out into the garden I was surprised to see Pete sitting at the breakfast table with Suzie, they were in deep conversation but on seeing me they both fell silent.

"Well good morning Chiquita" Pete got to his feet "did you sleep well?"

"Yes thank you" I answered as I sat down "you two looked as though you were cooking something up"

Reaching for the coffee pot Suzie muttered "not at all we weren't sure if you were up or not so I made Pete be quiet for a change" with this she gave a little laugh and looked at Pete for support.

"I hear that you are going to sea today" Pete countered skilfully changing the subject "if you had told me before I would have joined you" he wagged a finger at Suzie as if scolding her "but I'm always the last one to know what's going on" with that he stood "well it seems that I have a lot of work to do today, so I had better get on with it" he bent and kissed Suzie on the cheek "see you girls later, try to behave"

After he had left and when I felt the time was right I broached the subject of what I had seen "Suzie, earlier I thought I heard shouting was everything alright?" I looked at her over the rim of my coffee cup trying to gauge her reaction.

"Shouting? Are you sure it was here and not next door, they can be very noisy at times" I thought that I detected a slight edge to her voice and her hand shook a little as she lifted her cup of steaming coffee.

"Your most probably right or I might have dreamt it. I did drink rather a lot of rum last night" with that we both laughed and I felt the tension leave the air "so we are going to sea, please tell me not in a beautiful pea green boat like the owl and the pussy cat"

Suzie threw back her head and laughed "Oh Polly you do make me laugh. It is so wonderful to have you here. But we must get a move on Captain Tobias is a stickler for time"

I wasn't sure what to wear and on asking Suzie I was surprised to be told that everything that I would need would already be on the boat.

"Why don't you wait on the porch, enjoy the sunshine. I have a phone call that I need to make before we go" Suzie's voice still seemed a little edgy to me.

I did as she said and walked out to the porch and sat on the little swing seat with my eyes closed enjoying the early morning sun. The blasting of a car horn disturbed the peace and on opening my eyes was amazed to see a white stretch limousine parked outside of the gate. At the second blast of the horn Suzie came hurtling out of the door with a face as black as thunder.

"For god sake Jonathon, why don't you let the whole neighbourhood know that you're here" she scowled at him

The man muttered something under his breath "Sorry Polly, but what a scene. He can never arrive quietly" she smiled that sweet smile at me but I felt very unnerved by the events of this morning.

As we walked to the car Jonathon opened the door and I could hear the murmur of several woman's voices. On approaching the car to my surprise there were 6 young girls already seated, each were holding a glass of champagne.

Turning to Suzie I queried "Where are we going? I thought we were having a lazy day at sea?"

On hearing this the girls all erupted into laughter "Well I guess you may be lying down a lot" one of them answered and with that the others all hooted with laughter.

"Shut up Honey" Suzie snapped "Watch your mouth"

"Sorry, Sorry Suzie, it was only a joke" the girl now known as Honey meekly replied.

A very uneasy feeling swept through my body what the hell was going on "Suzie I don't think that I want to go out to sea today, maybe I'll stay in the garden and read" as I said this I noticed, from the corner of my eye, that the girls were all looking from Suzie and back to me as if waiting for something to happen.

"Oh, don't let Honey put you off she's always saying stupid things" Suzie gave her sweetest smile "come on jump in we need to be going" she paused "Chantelle pour Polly some champagne" stroking my hand she continued "I know that you will enjoy it"

During the journey Suzie introduced me to the girls "You already know that this one is Honey" she waved a hand in the direction of a stunningly beautiful girl. She was tall with long honey coloured hair. "Then we have Chantelle" this girl was picture perfect she looked as though she had been airbrushed, her skin shone like silk. She had short dark hair. "These three are from the left Christie, Princess and Belle" the first two were tall with legs that never seemed to stop, Belle was different she was shorter than the others and a little plump. "And lastly Tanya" the girl gave a little salute that sent the other five into giggles. Tanya had an athletic build and wore her hair in a tight afro.

"Lovely to meet you all, I will try to remember your names" I looked around the car at the six faces waiting for a reply, when none came I took a long gulp of my champagne.

The trip down to the port was breath-taking and on any other day I would have been blown away by the views, but today in the claustrophobic atmosphere of the limousine and with Honey's words echoing in my head I dreaded reaching our destination.

As we entered the dock gates we were waved straight through without being asked to stop. I noticed that all the other vehicles entering and exiting the port were stopped and the drivers asked for ID. Nothing seemed to be ringing true for me today.

Jonathon pulled the car to a stop alongside one of the biggest yachts in the dock, it looked more like a mini cruise ship than a yacht. As we walked up the gang plank I could see a tall tanned man pacing back and forwards on the deck. He seemed to be having a very animated conversation with someone. On seeing us board he quickly clicked his phone shut and walked towards us.

"Bloody hell Suzie, where the hell have you been? You should have been here half an hour ago" firstly glaring at Suzie with his hands on his hips, he then turned his attention to the rest of us. Looking each girl up and down until he got to me "Who's this? And what the bloody hell is she wearing?"

"Please don't be rude Tobias" Suzie looked embarrassed "this is Polly I told you about her, remember my friend from England"

"Friend or not get her out of those awful clothes immediately, our guests will be here soon" with that he started to climb the stairs to the wheel house "and for god's sake get the rest of them ready, they look as though they've been through a hurricane"

Clapping her hands Suzie barked orders "Chantelle redo your hair, Honey makeup, Christie hair and makeup. Princess, Belle and Tanya you look okay, get your dresses on and then get the champagne ready we can't serve it warm" turning to me "well you heard what the man said, this way" with that she walked off with me trotting behind.

"Suzie, please tell me what is going on? " I could feel the tears building in my eyes and sniffed to stop them falling.

"In here" she opened a door and there in front of us was the most sumptuous cabin that I had ever seen. The large bed was covered in a pale mint green silk throw that matched the curtains and as you walked your feet, literally, sank into the thick carpet. Next to the bed on a table was a bottle of champagne in a cooler with two crystal glasses that sparkled in the sunlight next to that was a silver box inlaid with mother of pearl.

Suzie had crossed to the other side of the cabin and was now pulling out various garments from the built in wardrobe "here put this on, this should be your size" she handed me a long cobalt blue halter neck dress "Polly please hurry the others will be here soon and I need to be up on deck to greet them. Where the fucking hell is Martha" She grabbed a phone that was on a table that stood at the other side of the bed "Get Martha down here now" she barked into the handset before slamming it down on the cradle "Polly don't just stand there get that dress on"

An older portly woman came hurrying into the cabin, she was dressed in a maids outfit "Sorry miss, I didn't know that you needed me" she sounded terrified.

"This is Polly" she nodded her head at me "get to work on her hair and makeup and please make it snappy we are running very late" smoothing down her own gown that had been stored in the wardrobe, Suzie crossed the cabin and before opening the door looked at the terrified maid "and Martha discretion, you understand"

Martha nodded her head "Please sit down Miss Polly, would you like your hair up or down" she ran her hand through my curls "Such pretty hair perhaps down"

I did as I was asked and as she started to comb and tease my curls into place I reached forward and picked up the lovely silver box. Turning it over in my hand to see the true beauty of the mother of pearl, I noticed that Martha was watching me with a strange look on her face "is everything alright?" I gently asked her.

"Miss, I know it's none of my business but do you know what you are here for?" she looked around the cabin as if she expected someone to jump out of the wardrobe.

"A party and a nice trip out to sea" was my reply "Suzie said good food and nice company. Why do you ask?"

"Open the box" Martha gestured to the lovely silver box that was still in my hand "when the girls use the cabins…" her voice became very quiet "well open it and you will see"

Slowly I lifted the lid unsure if I wanted to see what was inside "Oh my god!' was all I could say, the box was full of condoms. Snapping the lid shut I looked at Martha who was staring at my reflection in the mirror. Suddenly I felt sick and pushing Martha out of the way made a dash for the bathroom.

"Miss, Miss please come out, I will be in such trouble if I don't get you ready and up on deck soon" Martha's voice trembled as she spoke and I could tell that she was really frightened "please come out"

Sliding the lock open I walked out as steadily as I could back to the stool and sat down. My head was whirling surely Suzie didn't expect me to 'entertain' the men that would soon be on board. Seeing my worried face Martha gently spoke "Miss, don't worry I think that you are here to just make conversation with the guests, just like Miss Suzie does" she paused before continuing "I don't mean to be rude, but the men that come to these parties normally like their girls to be young" she blushed as she spoke "right you're ready, you look beautiful".

Chapter 6

Cautiously I stepped out into the sunshine. The deck at the stern of the yacht was packed with well-groomed men, they reeked of wealth. All but one, were casually dressed in well pressed shorts and polo shirts. From a glance I could tell from the cut of their clothes that they were very high end designer wear. Each was wearing the customary aviator sun glasses and huge diamond encrusted watch that glinted in the Caribbean sunshine.

To any casual onlooker this looked like your average boat party. The waiters ensuring that everyone's glass was constantly full and the men and girls laughing and chattering without, what seemed, to be a care in the world.

I noticed that the girls had all changed and were now in very short sexy dresses and all of them had bare feet. Their beautiful brown skin had a sheen that shone like silk, I guessed that this was through some type of oil, but the effect was breath-taking.

Suzie joined me in the doorway to the salon "I know that you have a million questions and I promise that I will answer each one, but later. Just enjoy today" she gestured to a waiter who had been patiently waiting a few feet away "Thomas will bring you my special concoction. Polly, listen to me, only drink what Thomas brings you" with that she handed me a glass of what I thought was champagne "it's made to look as though you have a glass of bubbly but it's really lemonade"

After taking a sip and waiting for Thomas to move away "Suzie, please tell me that you don't expect me to 'entertain' any of these gentlemen" I take a deep breath "I saw the contents of the box next to the bed"

"You must be mad! Of course not. We are here as chaperone's for the girls. We ensure that the men stick to the rules and don't abuse these lovelies" her eyes swept across the crowd "I'm going to introduce you to Don' she nodded at an older man sitting quietly in the corner at the rear of the yacht "he is very observant and will fill you in on some of the details. I'm afraid I must circulate"

I noticed that as we approached the man he straightened up from the semi slouched position he had been in and casually draped his arm across the top of the plush white cushions that were tightly nestled together on the seating area. He also had on the regulation aviator glasses and huge watch, but he was dressed in long cream trousers a dark blue shirt with a white and blue cravat at his neck.

"Don, I'd like to introduce you to my friend Polly. Do you mind if I leave the two of you to talk? "Without waiting for a reply she walked away.

"Well, nice to meet you Polly. Come and sit down" he gestured to the seat next to him "we have a birds eye view of all the activities from here. I'm told that you're from England, what part? If you couldn't guess I'm from Glasgow"

"Nice to meet you as well Don, I'm from Somerset" I tried to keep my voice as steady as possible but the tremor still came through.

"No need to be worried about me lassie, I'm not into all these shenanigans" he patted my hand as if to reassure me "have you any idea what's going on?"

I confirmed that I didn't "Didn't think so" he leaned in closer "these girls used to walk the streets and then one of them, Honey, landed a job in Suzie's beach side shop in Holetown. One day when Suzie was in the back of the shop doing the accounts, one of Honey's ex-customers happened to walk in and during their conversation asked Honey if she still did tricks! Once the man had gone Suzie called Honey to the office and asked her what it was all about" he took a sip of his champagne "Honey, was afraid that Suzie was going to sack her, but in fact she had given her boss a business idea"

"But surely if Honey had walked away from that sort of life, why would she want to go back?" to me this seemed like a backward step.

"Oh my dear innocent Polly, working the streets and doing this" he waved his hand in the direction of the party "is like two different worlds. These girls would have been turning tricks for a few dollars, but now, with the help of Suzie and her contacts, in an afternoon they can earn several thousand dollars!"

I nearly choked on my lemonade "What!" was all I managed to splutter.

"Indeed. These gentlemen will pay mega dollars for a party like this. Both you and Suzie will walk away today with…' he stopped and scratched his chin as he seemed to be weighing up the worth of the men on the yacht "somewhere in the region of $5000"

"$5000! But I haven't done anything to earn $2500, all I've done is sit here and talk to you" I was stunned at the amount and suddenly realised how rude I must have sounded "Sorry Don, I didn't mean just talked to you" I felt that I was digging a hole.

"No my lovely lassie, you misunderstand me $5000 each" my face must have been a picture as Don started to laugh a deep throaty Scottish rumble so rich was his laugh that I couldn't help but to laugh with him.

As the evening approached we were all summoned to the dining room, where a lavish meal of freshly caught lobsters, was served by Thomas. Captain Tobias joined the table bearing a platter of oysters and the largest dish of black caviar that I had ever seen.

After the meal we all retired to the salon where Marcus, one of the crew members, was entertaining us on the piano. My fears from earlier had just started to disappear, maybe Martha was wrong and my whole idea of what the girls were brought here for was nothing more than fear of the unknown.

With the champagne still flowing everyone was in very high spirits and a couple of the girls got up and started to dance. The men suddenly fell quiet as they watched with eager anticipation as the girls gyrated to the music. I had to admit that they really knew how to work their bodies, they seemed to be at one with the music.

I walked across to where Suzie was sitting on a high bar stool, we hadn't seen much of each other since she had left me with Martha in the cabin "What time does the party wrap up?" I asked as I climbed up onto the stool next to her.

"I'm afraid that's in the lap of the god's. I need to get these girls moving at this rate we'll still be here tomorrow morning" she spoke quietly "and I don't know about you but I need my beauty sleep" with that she beckoned to Chantelle who was standing by the piano tapping her long red fingernails on the shiny piano top to the music.

The girl immediately started to dance and as she did she moved towards a portly gentleman who was tapping his foot to the music. Wrapping her arms around his neck she whispered something in his ear and taking his hand lead him out of the salon.

"One down five to go" muttered Suzie

Within seconds of Chantelle leaving the room the rest of the men selected their favourite girls, leaving just Suzie, Don and me to listen to Marcus playing 'it's now or never' on the piano. On seeing Suzie stand, the music suddenly stopped and Marcus made himself scarce.

"Well, you old bugger" this was directed at Don, as Suzie flopped down on the sofa next to him "what have you been telling my friend?"

Don raised his glass and laughed that same rich deep laugh from earlier "the truth and nothing but the truth my lady" with that he tugged his forelock.

"Are you shocked?" she asked as she turned to face me.

"Shocked! Bloody hell yes I'm shocked! And I could truly do with something stronger than pigging lemonade!" I looked around to see what there was "Can I have champagne now or am I still on duty?" I asked with as much sarcasm as I could muster.

"Still on duty, I'm afraid. Until this lot shoot their load!" she threw her arm out in the direction of the salon door "hopefully with the skill of the girls it shouldn't be too long now. Tobias has already turned the yacht around so they had better get on with it or we will have the only rocking boat in the harbour" with that both she and Don laughed and in unison started to sing 'rock, rock, rock the boat' seeing the two of them swaying back and forward on the sofa as if rowing a boat I couldn't stop myself from joining in.

Once the yacht was safely moored and all of the men had been escorted to their respective cars, Suzie asked me to join her in the original cabin. On entering I couldn't believe my eyes, on the bed was thousands of dollars.

In her most business like voice Suzie instructed "right what we have to do is count this lot" she sat down on the edge of the bed "Polly, snap out of it we need to get counting otherwise we will be here all night"

Between us it didn't take long, sitting with my back against the giant mirror, which acted as a headboard, I exhaled and gave a small whistle "$50,000! WOW!"

"Now we have to divide this, let me see" Suzie started to mutter under her breath "$5000 for you" with that she pushed a pile of notes towards me "don't say anything Polly, this is how it is" turning back to the cash '$5000 for me, $5000 for Tobias, $5000 for Don...'

"Don! Don gets paid for being here?" now I really was confused

"My darling Polly, where do you think I get the men from? I supply the girls and he supplies the men. Now where was I?" shaking her head she went over the sums again"$20,000 taken care of, right now the girls. $4000 for Honey, $3000 each for the others' tapping her finger against her temple "what have I forgotten? Oh yes, £5000 to be shared between the crew members, hush money" she looked at me as she said this "that leaves $6,000 in the bank" clapping her hands she continued "that's what I call a good day's work"

The girls all seemed happy with their pay and left the yacht in very good spirits, we could hear their exciting talk of shopping trips as they piled into the waiting car.

We were the last to leave and as we walked down the gang plank I couldn't help but wonder what other surprises Suzie had in store for me. As my hand rested on the envelope of money nestled into my coat pocket an uneasy feeling crept over me.

After a fitful night's sleep I decided that I needed to talk to Suzie about the previous day's events. I found her sitting on the patio with a hot cup of coffee in her hand. She was dressed and from what she was wearing she looked as though she was ready to go out.

On seeing me she cheerfully called "hot coffee in the pot" sliding her sunglasses up onto her hair she added "my god Polly, you look as though you need a whole pot of coffee. Whatever is the matter?"

"Yesterday, yesterday is the matter!" I spat the words out.

"Grow up for god's sake! I thought you had more about you than worrying about a little party" She almost slammed her cup down on the table "you earned $5000 for doing nothing, what the hell is the matter with you?"

"What the hell is the matter with me? The matter with me is that I do not want to be a MADAM" I shouted the last word at her "even if this sits well with you Suzie it sure as hell doesn't with me" with that I took the envelope containing the money from my dressing gown pocket and threw it at her, before storming back into the house.

Chapter 7

I had moved into a hotel whilst I waited for my flight back to the UK. The only seat available was in two days' time and I thought that after my confrontation with Suzie it would be better to move out of her house. I had chosen to stay in a hotel that was just outside of Bridgetown, I didn't want to bump into Suzie, Pete or Don.

At last the day had arrived for me to leave, I was just about to climb into the taxi which I had booked to drive me to the airport when I heard my name being called. Turning in the direction of the voice I was surprised to see Thomas hurrying towards me.

"Miss Polly, Miss Polly wait please" by the time he reached the taxi he was out of breath and gasping for air "Miss Polly, Miss Suzie asked me to bring you this" he handed me a note. It read……

'My Darling Polly,

I am truly sorry that our friendship has ended this way and I hope that one day you will decide that I am not such a bad person.

I hope that you will accept this present as a thank you for your friendship.

Please don't hate me.

Love Suzie. Xx

I felt tears welling up in my eyes, how I wished that things had turned out differently. Without another word I took the box that Thomas held out to me and got into the taxi.

Once safely at the airport I opened the large white box to find the most exquisite dress. It was a deep red evening gown, with large diamante stones edging both the neckline and the hem, smaller stones glittered like little stars between the large stones. Holding it tightly to my chest I couldn't stop the tears.

The flight seemed to take forever but at last the seat belt light went on and we touched down at Gatwick. A huge sense of relief flooded over me, it would be good to be back home.

As we walked through the tunnel from the plane to passport control, we were all asked to form a single line so that the sniffer dogs could do their job. Without hesitation I stood behind a tall man and his smaller wife, as the dog worked his way down the line. The dog sniffed the man in front and then moved past me, just as I was about to walk after the others the dog back tracked and after sniffing my carry-on bag again immediately sat down. I smiled as I looked from the dog to the handler as I knew that I had nothing to worry about. Another security officer hurried forward and after a whispered conversation with the dog handler the officer turned to me.

"Please pick up your bag and follow me" his voice was pleasant and I did as I was asked "do you have luggage in the hold?"

"Yes" I was still smiling believing that I had nothing to worry about "just one case, it can't be missed it has huge butterflies on it".

I followed him to the baggage carousel where we retrieved my case "this way please" at this point he was joined by a female officer.

People had started to stare at me as if I was a criminal, which made me feel very uncomfortable. Trying to make polite conversation I sweetly asked "what seems to be the problem?"

Without answering the male officer pointed to a counter 'put your case and bag up here please. If it's locked please unlock it'

Another female officer had also joined us on our way to the counter and she now started going through my case. Unfolding and refolding everything as she took my items out. The male officer stepped forward when the case was empty and a swab was taken which they put into a machine, after a few moments the machine beeped.

The female officer then moved onto my carry-on bag lifting the dress, which I had carefully folded in the tissue paper from the box, she at last spoke "my, this is beautiful. It must have cost you a small fortune?"

I was so pleased that someone had eventually spoken to me that I stammered "it was a leaving present from my dear friend"

"Really? Well your friend must be very rich what does he do?" as she spoke she carefully folded the dress back into the tissue paper.

"No, not he, she" I smiled at the thought of a sugar daddy "she owns a number of boutique shops in the Caribbean"

Another swab was taken but this time the machine made a different noise, the officers both turned to me "have you been in contact with any drugs whilst you've been away?"

"Certainly not!" I spluttered

"Has anyone that you know smoked or taken any drugs around you" the female officer seemed to be looking for a reaction.

"No" after a pause "well not that I know of. I went to a party but I'm sure that there weren't any drugs there. It wasn't that sort of party"

"Oh really and what sort of party was it" the male officer's interest seemed to have been peaked by my statement.

"It was a yacht cocktail party. The guests there were very well to do. Not drug takers" I couldn't stop the indignation showing in my voice.

The officer shrugged "it's the ones that you don't think take drugs that very often do" his statement shook me. He turned to his colleague "get the statement chart" turning back to me he continued "we are going to proceed with a strip search" pausing "with your consent of course!"

By this time I couldn't be bothered to argue, all I wanted to do was to go home. The two female officers escorted me into a room and instructed me to take off my clothes and hand each item to them. When I was fully naked they told me to bend over and one of them opened my bottom cheeks, after which I was told to squat. On finding nothing I was allowed to get dressed.

As I walked out of the room I noticed the male officer in deep conversation with another man, they were both bent over my dress and seemed to be inspecting the diamante embellishment. On seeing me they both immediately straightened up and moved away from the counter.

"Mike, I folded that dress up so carefully" the female officer scolded the man that I hadn't met before "I'm so sorry miss, men honestly they have no idea of how delicate garments should be handled" she refolded the dress and placed it back in my carry-on.

"Can this lady go now" she addressed this to the man now known as Mike, he nodded his head "Thank you for your time and I apologise for any inconvenience that this has caused you"

With a great feeling of relief I picked up my bag from the counter and pulling my big case behind me made my way out of the customs area.

Chapter 8

I had been home for about 2 months when the parcel arrived. I remember that I was gardening when the delivery van pulled into the drive.

'Morning, parcel for Mrs Oakley' the driver seemed to be in a hurry 'leave it here for you Mrs" he shouted across the garden to me, as he put the parcel on the porch shelf. He jumped back in his van and sped out of the driveway before I had a chance to respond.

'I'm not expecting a parcel' I muttered to myself as I walked across the lawn towards the house. Picking up the parcel, which was quite large, I inspected the label and noticed that the postage was marked as Barbados 'I suppose that I might as well have a cup of tea, whilst I open you' I said to the parcel.

After the kettle had boiled and whilst my tea was brewing I took one of the sharp kitchen knives from the holder that stands next to the breadbin. Carefully prising off the tape I found a neatly wrapped package, with a note attached to it.

Hi Polly,

I hope that you don't mind but a friend of mine asked me to send a dress over as a surprise for his wife, as he doesn't want it to go to his address I suggested that he collects it from you. Please call him, number below, to let him know a convenient time for him to come.

Hope you are well.

Love you

Suzie xxxx

"The bloody cheek of the woman" I couldn't believe that after what had happened and as she hadn't even bothered to find out if I had arrived home safely, now she expected me to phone an unknown stranger and act as a bloody courier. Looking at the parcel I sighed "what can I do, you're here now. Let's phone the stupid man and get it over with"

I was about to put the receiver down when a gruff voice at the other end suddenly spoke "What!!" just that one word was spoken.

"Hello" I put on my poshest phone voice "can I speak to Mr Black?"

"It depends who you are" he spat back down the line.

"Oh, for god's sake, just get him on the phone" I couldn't stop the irritation in my voice, here I was minding my own business enjoying my gardening when all of a sudden I'm expected to deal with this rude idiot "tell him I've got a parcel for him"

"Oh, right sorry" the voice seemed to soften a little "this is Mr Black, sorry to be so rude but these bloody cold calls drive me nuts"

"Can you come and get this parcel today please" I didn't care about his cold calls all I wanted was to get back to my gardening.

"Yes, yes of course. Just a minute let me grab a pen and I'll jot down your address" I heard something being knocked over and him swearing before he came back on the line "okay let me have your address"

We arranged for him to come at 7.00 pm and I stated that I expected him to be punctual.

At exactly 7.00 pm a large white 4 x4 pulled into the driveway. I watched from an upstairs window as a middle aged man got out of the driver's side and walked towards the house. I noticed that he had quite a marked limp, at times he seemed to almost lose his balance.

"Most probably too proud to use a walking stick" I thought to myself as I watched him.

I slowly walked down the stairs as the front door bell sounded, after all why should I rush. As I got to the foot of the stairs I bent and picked up the parcel as the bell rang again.

"Here you are" I said as soon as I opened the door "Please ask Suzie not to send your parcels here in the future. If you don't want your wife to see them I would suggest you arrange a post office box" with that I started to shut the door.

"Suzie, who the bloody hell is Suzie!" The man's foot jammed open the door so that it was impossible for me to close it "what the hell are you talking about, I don't have a wife!"

"Whatever, just don't have your parcels delivered here again. Now either get your foot out of the way or face the consequences" with one look at my angry face he withdrew his foot and started to hobble away. "Hang on a minute" his words had just sank into my brain "what do you mean, who the hell is Suzie? She sent the parcel, didn't she?"

"Like I said who the bloody hell is this Suzie? Never heard of her. Pete sent this parcel" he started to walk away "and like I said I don't have a bloody wife or a bloody mistress"

Before I could say anything else he had got into his car, throwing the parcel onto the back seat and was reversing out of the drive, leaving me standing at the open door wondering just what the hell was going on.

As he drove away I noticed a black saloon car, pull out from the side road opposite and drive off in the same direction as he had gone, but this was nothing unusual as the road was always quite busy.

As I walked back down the hall towards the sitting room I stopped next to the phone table and wondered if I should try to speak to Suzie to find out what was going on. I decided not to as to be honest I didn't really want to know. The parcel had been delivered and that was the end of it. Or so I thought.

Chapter 9

I had enjoyed the last couple of carefree weeks, doing the round of garden centres and taking in a few plays at the local theatre, the parcel episode seemed a long time ago.

This particular day I had spent a good few hours at a local National Trust property and on the way back had decided to treat myself to a Chinese takeaway. The wonderful aroma of my Chinese dumplings, orange chicken, fried rice and egg rolls, had nearly driven me crazy in the car on the way home. As I dished it up my stomach made a loud rumble that made me laugh. I suddenly thought of Steve, he would be very angry at such a childish reaction.

The shrill sound of the phone ringing brought me sharply back to the present "if that's a cold call!" I angrily said to myself as I snatched up the receiver "YES" I almost shouted down the line.

"Whoa, someone having a bad day?" a gravelly male Scottish voice rumbled at the other end of the line "Is this a bad time Polly" this was followed by a familiar deep laugh.

A shiver ran down my back "Don? Don is that you?"

"Last time I checked. But seriously is this a bad time?" Don's voice had softened.

"Well it is and it isn't. It's nice to hear from you" I lied as convincingly as I could manage "I've just served up my dinner and I'm starving"

"Promise I won't keep you long" he paused as if waiting for me to object when I kept quiet he continued "I'm in the UK, well in London actually and I would love to see you" I heard a clink of a bottle against a glass "would you be able to come up for a few days"

"Um, I'm not sure if that's a good idea" I felt torn as a few days in London would be lovely but I was wary of his motives.

Hearing the hesitation in my voice he turned on the charm "I have a penthouse suite with a magnificent view over the city" pausing for a moment "I promise to be a good boy" laughing he finished "promise no hanky panky!"

"Well why not I haven't been to London for a while and some retail therapy would do me the world of good" as soon as I had said it I wished that I could retract my statement.

"Brilliant. I'll send my driver to collect you first thing in the morning" he genuinely sounded delighted "Oh, bring your passport I have a private jet at my disposal so we may fancy a little jaunt" without waiting for an answer the line went dead.

Walking back into the kitchen the smell of my takeaway suddenly made my stomach turn. Scraping it into the kitchen bin I had a sinking feeling in the pit of my stomach, what had I just agreed to and why do I need to take my passport?

After a sleepless night I stumble around the bedroom trying to get organised and select several outfits that are not too formal but also not too casual. As I click the locks of my suitcase shut I hear the crunch of car wheels on the driveway, tentatively I peep out of the bedroom window "Bloody hell, this is madness" I mutter under my breath as I stare down at a gleaming black Rolls Royce. As soon as the car pulls to a stop the driver immediately jumps out, my head starts to reel as I peer at the driver "Jonathon!" I shake my head in bewilderment as I ask myself "what the hell have I agreed to?"

Slowly I make my way down the stairs to the hall as the sound of the doorbell being rung persistently rings in my ears. Plastering on what I hope is a convincing smile I open the door "Well, this is unexpected. How are you Jonathon?"

"Fine thank you miss and you? Are you ready for your great adventure?" with that he picks up the case that is sitting at my feet "we had better get moving miss, or we'll get snarled up in the rush hour traffic" as he turns away I'm sure that I see a smirk on his young dark face.

I decide not to ask him for any details, as I'm sure that I won't get a truthful answer. Instead I settle into the fine leather upholstery and enjoy the ride. As we glide down the high street the car draws a few stares from people hurrying about their business, at which point I'm glad that the rear windows are blacked out. Before long we head onto the motorway and Jonathon puts his foot down as we speed towards London.

Again for the second time in 24 hours I think of Steve, always a careful driver. Whenever we travelled on the motorway his comments would always be the same "Look at this bloody idiot" or "I'm doing 70 so what the hell speed is he doing" on and on he'd drone. I was always glad when we got back onto the normal 'A' roads. I wonder if she feels the same way! After all the honeymoon period would now be over and perhaps she's seeing him without the rose tinted glasses.

At some point I must have drifted off to sleep as the next thing that I am aware of is Jonathon's voice "Miss, miss" his voice sounded urgent, as I opened my eyes I realised that we were parked outside of a very swanky hotel "Miss, we're here" holding out his gloved hand in my direction "please let me help you"

"No, just a minute" fumbling in my handbag I found my mirror "Oh dear god" I exclaimed as I saw the sight staring back at me. My hair that had been held in a perfect bun but was now half out and my makeup was smudged. As quickly as I could I tidied my hair and applied some powder, smoothing down my now wrinkled dress I alighted, with as much dignity as I could muster, from the car.

"Good Morning Madam" the liveried doorman stepped forward and taking my suitcase from Jonathon opened the heavy steel and glass entrance door, which led into the foyer "Mr McKinter, is expecting you" with that the man passed my suitcase to one of the bellhops and I was ushered to a private lift that was situated discreetly in a corner of the foyer.

I don't think that I have ever been in such a quiet lift, the slightest of hums emanated from the workings. Three sides of the lift was decorated with a very opulent black and gold design, whilst the other wall was completely glass.

"Good job I'm not afraid of heights" I quipped to the young bellhop who was accompanying me, but he made no reply and just gave a slight nod of his head. As we ascended the view from the lift was truly magnificent as you could see right across the city. If I hadn't been so apprehensive about the reason for my visit, I would have truly enjoyed the ride. But all too soon the lift stopped and the doors slid open.

"Thank goodness, you're here at last" Don was standing in front of the lift, coffee cup in one hand "it's okay laddie" he took the case from the young bellhop "I'll see to the lady from here" as he spoke he tucked a couple of notes into the boys top pocket. "Sorry to say this but you look a mess" he was looking me up and down "why don't you have a shower and then we can start our adventure"

"Well, nice to see you to Don!" I was now on the brink of tears this was all too much "both you and Jonathon have called this little 'holiday' an adventure, I take it that all will be explained"

"Oh my dear girl" Don took my hand as he spoke "nothing to worry about, just a turn of phrase. Now go and get that shower, I don't know about you but I'm ready for food"

Within an hour we were sitting opposite each other in a lovely little bistro that overlooked the Thames. As I watched the boats silently sweep by a thought suddenly struck me "Did Suzie ask you to contact me?"

"Yes and no" Don paused as he poured us both a glass of wine "she wants to get back in touch with you, but is unsure of the reception that she'll get" he hesitated as the waiter placed our food in front of us "what she does isn't so bad. If those girls had stayed on the streets they would either be dead or most probably riddled with some dreadful disease! With Suzie looking after them they have a nice income and very good medical cover" raising his wine glass to his lips "you shouldn't think badly of her"

"Maybe or maybe not, I just think that instead of telling me she just assumed that I would go along with it all" I kept my eyes firmly fixed on my plate as I spoke "if she had explained it I might have reacted differently" swallowing hard to stop the sob that was rising in my throat "I miss her"

"And she misses you" Don reached across the little table and covered my hand with his "just for today lets enjoy the sunshine and each other's company" lifting his glass again "let's toast friendship" dropping his voice to a near whisper "tomorrow I need to run some thoughts past you, but as I said let's enjoy today"

Chapter 10

The smell of cooked bacon roused me from my sleep, for a moment I can't get my bearings and panic sets in, until Don's voice drifts through the partly open bedroom door, it sounds as though he is having an argument with someone "I know, I know but for god sake give me some credibility for having a brain" it goes quiet for a moment, he's obviously talking to someone on the phone "let me handle things my way" again a pause "I'll speak to you later"

Pulling my dressing gown around me I step out into the large sitting room "Morning" I brightly say "I would have said good morning but from the sound of your phone call maybe not!"

"Oh that was nothing" he walks over to the dining table and pulls out a chair, indicating for me to sit down "I thought we would have a civilised full English" with that he takes a plate covered with a silver dome and puts it in front of me.

Once he has settled himself and is heartily tucking into his breakfast I broach the subject of what he wants to talk to me about. Placing his knife and fork back on his plate he leans back and sighs "Can't we just enjoy our breakfast" picking up his coffee cup he takes a sip of the scolding liquid "I would prefer to talk to you whilst I show you something"

"Why has everything got to be so mysterious?" I push my chair away from the table and start to stalk towards my bedroom "I will be ready in 30 minutes and you had better be ready to start talking"

Dead on 30 minutes I walk back into the sitting room to find Don waiting for me "The car's waiting, my lady" with that he gives a slight bow which makes me smile "I'm sorry if you think that I'm being mean to you, but once we get there you will see why it's easier to do things my way"

The London traffic is worse than I had remembered, even with the congestion charge, the traffic was still bumper to bumper. Jonathon seemed to know his way around, which surprised me. He would suddenly peel out of the traffic and speed down a side road. At last the car came to a halt outside a small mall of what looked like very swanky shops.

Jonathon jumped out of the car and ran around to my side to open the door for me, as I stepped out onto the pavement a man came rushing out from a nearby shop doorway "Good Morning, you must be Mrs McKinter"

Before I could answer Don intercepted "I'm Mr McKinter, where is Julian? He was supposed to meet us this morning"

"I'm so sorry sir, Julian sends his apologies he has been called away" as the man spoke he started to fumble with the bunch of keys that he was holding "I'm Christian. Julian has given me the low down on what you are looking for. Shall we!" with that he turned and walked back towards the now empty doorway.

As we enter the shop, Christian flicks on lights and starts talking rapidly about the desirability of the shop and the area, and how not many premises of this size come onto the market. I can see from Don's face that he is not impressed that this Julian character has stood us up "Look I don't mean to be rude, but can you just be quiet" he glares at the younger man "I don't need a lecture on the area" the young man looks as though he is about to cry "why don't you do something useful and go and get us all a coffee" with that he takes out his wallet and shoves a £20 note into the man's hand.

"You are bloody rude" I hiss at him when Christian has scuttled out of the door in search of coffee "and why are we in a bloody empty shop?"

By now Don has disappeared through a door at the back of the empty space "come here" he shouts "this is going to be perfect"

"Perfect for what?"

"Suzie wants to start importing some of her dresses. This location will be perfect. Look at all of this storage space. That room can be done out as a VIP area, to allow the more privileged some privacy"

"You've brought me up to London because Suzie wants to import dresses!" I try to keep my voice as calm as possible "what the bloody hell has that got to do with me?"

Just as he was about to answer we hear the door to the shop open "I'll talk to you after this idiot has gone" Don inclines his head to the now approaching Christian "We'll take it. Get Julian to drop the contracts off at the hotel today" taking my arm he adds "and I do mean TODAY" with that he steers me out of the door and into the waiting car.

"Don, I really need to know what is going on and what this has got to do with me?" I catch Jonathon watching Don in the rear view mirror and I'm sure that the two of them are up to no good.

"No problem" he pats my hand as if he is talking to a child "Jonathon I think that a nice little quiet pub would do nicely for lunch. Do you know of anywhere?" Jonathon just nods and we head off out of the city.

'The Quiet Woman" inn is lovely, it's set right on the river next to a lock gate with house boats tethered along the river bank, they're all painted in bright colours and remind me of the travellers caravans, that I used to watch as a child, when they came to my village when the fair was in town. Suddenly Cher's song 'Gypsy's, Tramps and Thieves' starts playing in my head. As we take our seats next to the large picture window I wish that I could enjoy this beautiful setting, but my heart is feeling very heavy and the feeling of doom is rising in my stomach.

"Okay, I think that you have been kept in the dark long enough" Don takes a slurp of his beer "the reason why I have brought you to London is Suzie wants you to be the CEO of her new import business, here in the UK. She needs someone that she can trust and from what she's told me you more or less ran your ex-husbands firm, at least at the beginning"

"No, no I don't want to live in London and run some dress shop!" the thought of leaving my lovely house and garden makes me shudder "you can tell her to forget it"

Holding up his hand Don continues "Now wait and listen to what I have to say. You wouldn't need to live in the city fulltime once the shop was up and running and reliable staff had been found" pouring me another glass of wine he leaned across the table "this could be very lucrative for you. The dresses that Suzie wants to import are one off originals, unique to the fortunate ladies who would buy them, they will sell for thousands"

"Good for Suzie" I start to protest but the look on Don's face makes me stop.

"No, not good for Suzie, but good for you!" he looks out of the window as a young couple walk past arm in arm "the deal comes with a penthouse apartment and 25% of the company profits plus, of course, a very generous salary"

Our food finally arrives, but I seem to have lost my appetite and as Don tucks into his steak I just sit and look at my plate "Something doesn't seem right" I look up at Don and again I think that I catch that same look on his face that I had seen pass between him and Jonathon in the car earlier.

Chapter 11

The next morning as I opened the bedroom curtains the sky is heavy with that horrible misty rain, the whole city seemed to have a grey cloak of doom thrown over it. Looking in the long mirror to the right of the window I shudder, another sleepless night is not doing my face any favours.

Slowly I walk into the shower and let the warm water run over my body, I wish that it could wash away this feeling of foreboding that is creeping ever deeper into my brain. Pulling on a pair of cream trousers and a blue top I tie my hair up into a loose bun, which saves me from having to spend ages drying it. I seem to be doing everything in slow motion today and realise that I am in no hurry to see Don this morning. After a while I know that I cannot put it off any longer so pulling my shoulders back I walk out into the sitting room.

As I enter the room Don is already sitting at the dining room table enjoying another hearty breakfast. The smell of the food makes me feel quite queasy and I opt just for a strong cup of coffee. Looking at the man opposite me over the rim of my coffee cup "Well what surprises do you have for me today?" as I speak he places his knife and fork with a clatter back onto his now empty plate.

"Now that you mention it" he lifts his cup to his lips and takes a gulp of his tea "you did bring your passport with you, didn't you?"

"My passport! Yes I have it, why?"

"Good" he smiles "the surprise today is that we are going to see Suzie"

"What! If you think that I am flying out to Barbados you have another........." I stop as he starts to laugh that same deep Scottish laugh that I first heard on the yacht "I don't know why you're laughing I don't think that it's very funny"

"My dear girl, I only have a small private plane at my disposal not a bloody jumbo jet" he tries to stifle his laugh "of course we're not going to Barbados but we are going to the Channel Islands. Now stop wittering and go and pack, we will be there for a couple of days"

Within the hour we are sitting on the runway at Gatwick waiting for our flight slot. From the way that Don had described it I was expecting a little four seater bone shaker, but in fact it was one of the plushest planes that I had ever flown in. The seats, 10 in all, are cream leather recliners, perfect I should imagine for longer flights. Don had told me on the way to the airport that our flight would take less than an hour, so we would be in Jersey for lunch. As soon as we are airborne Jonathon, who seemed to be acting as the steward, serves coffee and hot croissants.

I look across the aisle at Don who is tapping away on his mobile phone "Don" when he didn't respond I almost shout "DON!"

"What?" still looking at his phone "Look relax, everything will become clear. Stop fretting" he sounds annoyed and keeps frowning at the screen of his phone.

Before long we are instructed to buckle up and the plane starts its descent. Looking out of the little oval window I wonder what on earth is waiting for me down there.

Stepping off of the plane I am amazed at the climate, for some reason I had expected it to be really warm but a shiver runs down my back. Don takes hold of my arm and steers me towards an electric cart that is waiting to take us to the arrivals building. The arrival process is very quick and as we walk out of the airport, I am glad to see Jonathon is already standing next to a black SUV. He quickly loads our luggage and we set off on our short journey.

The journey itself only takes half an hour and we are soon sweeping up the drive to the stone and tile farmhouse that Suzie has rented. The house is set in a beautiful garden with a little sun terrace looking out to sea. My heart skips a beat as a familiar figure walks out of the open French doors. As soon as the car comes to a halt and Jonathon opens the door for me Suzie rushes forward arms outstretched "Oh Polly, it's so good to see you I wasn't sure if you would come!"

I want to hold back from her but emotion takes over and I fall into her arms "It's lovely to see you to" I whisper in her ear, holding her away from me, I continue "but I still don't really know why I'm here and why all the cloak and dagger stuff"

Taking my hand she gently pulls me towards the house "I thought that you would all be hungry so I thought to welcome you to Jersey you might like an authentic Jersey meal" we enter the house through the open French doors and are greeted by the most wonderful smell "this is Mrs A'Court" a little plump lady is standing at the far side of the table "she has prepared lunch of Bean Crock followed by Jersey Wonders"

Mrs A'Court beamed with pride as she muttered "Bouonjour" when she noticed the blank look on our faces she added "Good Morning, I hope that you had a pleasant flight" turning to Suzie "the meal needs about another hour. Can I leave you to serve it? I need to get back" when Suzie confirmed that it was fine the woman departed with a cheery "A betot"

As soon as the meal was ready we all took our seats at the big wooden farmhouse table and the meal was absolutely sensational "Mrs A'Court certainly knows how to cook" Don mumbled between mouthfuls "I can see why you asked her to cater for the do?" this was directed at Suzie.

"Do! What do?" I looked from Suzie to Don and back again "No-one told me anything about a do!"

"Oh for god sake Don, please tell me that you asked Polly to bring the dress" Don looked dumbfounded for a moment "Bloody hell I ask you to do one little thing and you balls that up!" Suzie's eyes darted from Don to me "Sweetie I don't suppose that you by chance brought that lovely dress that I sent to you when you left Barbados, did you?"

"No sorry, I didn't know that there was going to be an occasion" I could feel the hostility now dancing in the air in the room between Don and Suzie "When is this do anyway?"

"Tomorrow evening" Suzie stated flatly leaning back in her chair as she started to drum her fingers on the table "Is Margaret looking after your house Polly?" I confirmed that she was "Would you be able to phone her and ask her to give the dress to Jonathon, he could fly back and pick it up" looking back at Don "although by rights I should make you do it!"

"Is it really that important that she wears that bloody dress, you have a few dozen up there" with that Don nodded his head towards the staircase that lead to the first floor "I don't really want the plane going back and forward, for nothing" stopping he leaned forward "we don't want to arouse any unwanted attention, do we?"

Suzie let out a long sigh "I suppose so, but that dress was especially beautiful" pushing her chair back from the table she stood up and holding out her hand to me "come on, let's go outside and I'll explain about tomorrow"

"Jonathon, can you bring wine and some nibbles out to the terrace please" Suzie still holding my hand strolled towards the open doors "Let's sit out here and enjoy the view"

As soon as we were seated she started to talk "Along with exporting some of my dresses to the UK we thought" at this she indicated herself and Don "that Jersey would be a good location, plenty of money on the island and although I concede there are some decent shops" she gave a little sniff "nothing that can hold a candle to our dresses. So we have arranged a little cocktail party for some of the wealthy island ladies here tomorrow evening, obviously with their husbands. " Lifting her face to the late afternoon sun "the girls are flying in early tomorrow morning and they will act as our models"

"The girls? What girls?" I felt that same uneasy feeling rising in my stomach.

"Honey and the rest. Funny they didn't need to be asked twice" Suzie laughed "especially when they knew that there would be some very, and I mean very wealthy gentlemen on hand"

"Aren't you forgetting that their wives will be there to" but this just made Suzie and Don laugh even more.

"My sweet, sweet Polly these girls are masters of their art, if these guys don't off load bundles of cash on these girls then I'm going to retire" she indicated to Jonathon to pour the wine "these poor suckers haven't seen anything as exotic or erotic as my girls in full flow, their poor wives don't stand a chance"

The girls flew in early the following day. Jonathon drove Suzie and I to the airport to meet them, I'm not sure that Jersey had ever seen anything like it. I thought that the security men's eyes would pop out of their heads. Honey was the first to walk through arrivals, she had made sure that her long slender legs were fully on show with her short mini dress just covering her curvy bottom. Christie, Princess and Belle had all opted for knee length shorts teamed with very fitted tops that showed off their ample cleavages. The last two to emerge were Tanya and Chantelle, they were dressed almost identically in very tiny shorts and little crop tops, the whole ensemble left very little to the imagination.

I noticed that Suzie was smiling in a very satisfied way and on seeing me looking at her simply said "That's my girls. I told them to make sure that they made an entrance and as entrances go that sure as hell is one"

We made our way slowly towards the exit watching as the girls worked their audience. Honey was a master of the shy but come hither look, she would single out a man and dropping her head slightly would give him the full blast of her big brown eyes from beneath her lashes. The men didn't stand a chance and you could visibly see them go weak at the knees.

Once all of us were seated Jonathon slid the limousine door closed. The girls all looked at each other and all started to sing the Abba song "Money, money, money"

Laughing Chantelle waved a hand in Honey's direction "If you don't hook some decent bread girl then the world aint round" The rest of the girls all joined in with comments back and forth between each other.

By the time that we arrived back at the farmhouse the workmen had arrived and were erecting the large white marquee on the front lawn. There seemed to be people everywhere bustling in and out of the house. Local woman, who I assumed were helpers of Mrs A'Court, were busy arranging huge flower displays that would adorn both the entrance to the marquee and the centre of the round tables that guests would be seated at during the meal and subsequent fashion show. As the limousine came to a halt on the gravel driveway the whole place suddenly went quiet with all eyes on the car.

"Well baby girls I think that this is our time to shine" Honey slicked on some extra lip gloss and tossing her hair smirked "let's show these locals what glamour is all about" with that she allowed Jonathon, who was standing at the open car door, help her to step out into the sunshine. I swear that there was an audible gasp from the assembled woman as Honey straightened up and started to wiggle, on her five inch heels, towards the farmhouse closely followed by the other five who were all making sure to strut their stuff.

They all reached the open French doors just as Mrs A'Court walked out carrying a tray of cold drinks. I honestly thought that the poor woman was going to faint. Luckily Don had walked out behind her and deftly took the tray from her and expertly steered her to a nearby chair.

"Well hi sweetie" Honey bent down, making sure that the workmen had a good view of her legs "Sorry if we startled you. Are these drinks for us?" Mrs A'Court seemed unable to speak and just nodded.

By now Suzie had joined the group on the terrace and gently patted the older woman's arm "I'm sure that the drinks are much appreciated" Suzie pulled a chair up and sat next to the woman "these lovelies are the models for tonight. Let me introduce you" as she announced each name the girl would do a little twirl ensuring that the workmen had full view of their antics "now girls I think that you should all retire to your rooms and get some rest, I need you all to look your best tonight" turning to look across the lawn to where work on the marquee had stopped "and I need that lot to get on with their work"

Dutifully the girls all followed Jonathon into the house and disappeared from sight. At last Mrs A'Court seemed to find her voice "Dear God, I think that you had better put the local paramedics on standby" she stood up and straightened her apron "there may be some heart attacks tonight" walking away she quietly muttered "I'm glad that Mr A'Court isn't coming!"

The day wore on with the sound of hammering as the marquee was finished and a wooden floor was laid. The ladies busied themselves with the flowers and when it was all finished it really did look beautiful. Standing in the entrance to the marquee Suzie and I were amazed at how they had managed to do so much in such a short time "it looks beautiful. If this doesn't ensure that you get the orders you need then nothing will!"

"No my lovely, don't you mean if we don't get the orders that we deserve" Suzy turned and hugged me "after all you are my CEO" holding me away from her she continued "let's go and supervise these girls and then we can get ready ourselves"

Once everyone had been inspected and was deemed to be ready Suzie stood in the middle of the large sitting room "now listen all of you, I do not want any of you seen by our guests until the fashion show" at this she looked around the room "I need you all to be on your best behaviour tonight, no drinking before the show" at this there was a group groan "I mean it! If I find that any of you have had even a sip of champagne there will be trouble with a capital T and we all know what that means, don't we?" the question hung in the air "right, now that's sorted you all have your own rack of dresses so no dawdling between outfits. Remember the more orders we get the bigger your bonus. So my lovelies work those bodies, but don't alienate the wives, you can do that in your own time"

As we walk out of the room we hear the first crunch of tyres on the gravel driveway. Don who is walking behind us mutters "Well here we go"

The girls all work the floor with grace and just the right amount of sexiness thrown in. I find it hard to imagine the majority of the middle-aged and somewhat portly wives in these very slinky dresses, but as Suzie points out that's not our problem, if they believe that they will look as good as the models then let them have that dream. The wine flows freely, as do the orders which makes the night a huge success.

At the end of the night the girls all line up at the entrance of the marquee to wish our guests a safe journey and I am surprised to see that most of the men slip the girls money and I don't mean a note or two but in most cases quite a wad! Later when we are all drinking a celebratory glass of champagne the talk turns to the money "Bloody hell, I've made £3000 just for saying goodnight" Princess says as she waves the money in the air "what about the rest of you?"

Honey and Chantelle look at each other and burst out laughing "Should we tell them?" Honey buries her head in Chantelle's hair as they both rock with laughter.

"What? Come on you can't leave it like that!" Princess looks at Suzie "Do you know what they're on about?" Suzie shakes her head "Come on you two, let us all into the joke!"

Chantelle wipes tears of laughter from her face and without looking at Honey and trying not to laugh she starts "The old guy on table five slipped Honey a note half way through the night" stifling her giggles "he wants Honey and me to meet him……" laughing now she looks at the girl next to her "I can't you'll have to tell them"

"He wants us to meet him…. Oh God, for a threesome" again both girls dissolve into giggles "he's willing to pay us" stopping she looked around at the expectant crowd "£10,000 if we will spend the night with him on his boat"

"No, I will not allow it" at the sound of Suzie's voice the room falls quiet "Do you hear me, I will not allow it!"

"No, you misunderstand Suzie we're not laughing because he wants to pay us we're laughing because of the fact that he passed the note to his wife to give to us" Honey suddenly sounded a little frightened "we know that one of the rules is no threesomes"

I was left totally mystified, they seemed to do everything else so why no threesomes, it was something that I would ask Suzie about when we were alone.

I was woken early the next morning to the sound of banging coming from the garden. Grabbing my robe I walked across the bedroom and pulled back the curtains to see the workmen had arrived and were now dismantling the marquee. Just as I was about to turn away I caught sight of Suzie and Don standing at the end of the stone terrace, they seemed to be either having a row or discussing something animatedly. Suzie had her hands on her hips and was leaning with her face very close to Don's, I guessed from her stance that it had to be a row.

Quickly I dressed and made my way down stairs. On reaching the ground floor I could see the two of them standing in the same place on the terrace, as I walked out into the early morning sunshine Suzie turned towards me "Thank god, someone with some sense!" as I walked towards them she continued "will you please tell this idiot man that it's not a good idea"

As I joined them Don folded his arms across his chest and very grumpily stated "Two against one that's not fair"

"Well how do you know that I will be on Suzie's side" I looked from one to the other "is someone going to tell me what all the fuss is about"

Suzie glanced across to where the workmen were loading the parts of the marquee onto the back of their lorry and in a hushed voice continued "He thinks that the girls should take some of these numbskull men up on their offers and I've told him that it's a really bad idea as the whole point of coming onto Jersey is to have low key bolthole" she paused for a moment "you know just in case"

"By numbskulls I take it you mean the men from last night?" this was confirmed by a nod of her head "Well for a start I didn't know there had been any serious offers of anything, obviously discounting the stupid threesome idea"

Don pulled one of the heavy wrought iron chairs from under the table and sat down heavily on it "Several of the guests approached me and asked if the girls gave 'private shows" he gestured in Suzie's direction "but madam here doesn't think that's a good idea. I think that we should let the girls decide so that's where you come in"

"I'm sorry Don but I have to agree with Suzie, the girls all have return tickets for later today and I think that they should be on that plane" he let out a loud sigh "after all it might make these gentlemen persuade their wives that a return fashion show is needed" I patted his arm and winked at him "you know this type of man is used to getting what he wants immediately, so if they have to wait, up goes the anticipation and up goes the price"

Don let out one of his loud raucous laughs "you know you may be right" looking at Suzie he smiled "we'll make a business woman out of her yet!"

Suzie clapped her hands and stated "Now that's settled breakfast is calling"

Later that day when the girls had been dispatched back to Barbados and Suzie and I were sitting enjoying the late afternoon sun I broached the subject with her of the 'special dresses' "Suzie there's one thing that I don't understand" as I spoke Don joined us with Jonathon following carrying a bottle in one hand and a tray in the other "You both keep referring to some of the dresses as special, but I don't quite understand"

The wine that Jonathon had now poured for us truly hit the spot and I was glad that he had brought out some crackers and cheese to soak it up. "I think that it is about time for all of the mystery to be lifted, about these special dresses" I stated looking from Suzie to Don "If the dress that you gave to me is anything to go on and they are all as lovely as that then, in my opinion, they are all special dresses.

"You're right" Suzie placed her half full glass back onto the table "as you know from what Don has already shown and told you, I want to import some of my more special dresses to the UK. We want to be able to supply the wealthy with what they want" at this point she glanced at Don "We have found that if we spray the underskirt of some of our more desirable dresses we can charge a lot more for them"

"Spray? Spray them with what?" I noticed that Don and Jonathon, who was standing in the doorway, both had that look on their faces again a look that I didn't like.

Before Suzie could answer Don interrupted "One of the men that Honey knows has a ………" He pauses and seems to be trying to think of the right words to use "a chemical company and he has come up with this idea of using a spray to enhance the longevity of some materials"

"I don't understand why that's necessary, these rich woman would only want to wear a dress once" this whole situation and explanation didn't quite ring true. "No I'm sorry but there has to be more to it than you're telling me"

"You're right" Suzie was now glaring at Don "Preserve material what a load of rubbish! She's not a fool, don't treat her like a fool" Looking back at me she continued "he has come up with a formula to spray liquid gold onto material, so that when it gets to its destination it can be turned back into solid gold"

"But why?" I still couldn't see the point.

"You remember the dress that was sent to you that Mr Black collected, well that was a prototype" Suzie seemed to be studying my reaction "and it worked. Look, I know that you said that you don't want to go to Barbados but I think that you should see how the process works"

"Maybe I'm being stupid but why do you need to liquefy gold just to turn it back into its solid form" I feel so confused, is it me or has the wine addled my brain.

At this Don pushed back his chair, placing both of his hands on the table he leaned into my face "for god's sake Polly don't be so thick" with that he abruptly turned away and disappeared with Jonathon into the house.

Chapter 12

After 2 days of Suzie's constant nagging I agreed to go back to Barbados. The flight seemed to take no time at all and as the plane wheels screeched to a halt that same old feeling of foreboding resurfaced in my brain.

Leaving the aircraft the heat hit me and I grabbed at the metal hand rail to steady myself, that familiar sick feeling was starting in my stomach, what the hell was I thinking when I agreed to come back here. On reaching the ground I follow the other passengers towards the buses that are waiting to transport everyone to the arrivals terminal. At this point I think of the trips that I had taken in the past with Steve.

He would always, and not in a quiet voice moan "Like being a load of cattle herded off the plane and on to these disgusting crowded buses. Jammed in with sweaty irritable people" He seemed to forget that he was one of these sweaty irritable people, that irony always escaped him.

Once all of the normal airport formalities had been completed, baggage collection, passport control and my least favourite of all customs I was very glad to see Jonathon waiting for me in the arrivals hall. As soon as he saw me he quickly walked forward and taking my suitcase in one hand he steered me skilfully through the throng of newly arrived people towards the exit. Once outside he stopped next to a big white SUV, opening the door he ushered me into the back seat, after stowing my case safely in the car's boot we speed away from the airport.

Before long we had arrived at Suzie's home, looking at me she smiled "I didn't think that you would mind staying with me" with a shrug she continued "I promise no yacht parties"

"It's fine" a little part of me was relieved as I really didn't want to stay in a hotel on my own, I would have too much time to think.

The house was just as I had remembered it being bright, light with a welcoming factor and without thinking I found myself smiling. Suzie was already in the kitchen bustling about. I could hear cupboards being opened and shut and the sound of chopping. For a few seconds I stood quietly in the kitchen doorway watching her until she spoke "Well don't just stand there, get the cook a drink"

The evening started well, we enjoyed a lovely fresh salad which was washed down with quite a few rums. "Suzie, something has been bothering me"

"What" she reached across and refilled my glass. I noticed that her hand shook just a little, but I put it down to the rum.

"I don't understand why Don got so angry when I questioned the spraying of the gold" I could almost hear her brain working as I pressed on "after all if I am to be a partner or part owner of this enterprise then surely I should be in possession of all of the facts"

"You're right, of course. Don gets a bit defensive when he's not getting his own way immediately" she took a long drink of her rum "he feels that the less you know the better for you" she put her glass down and leaning back in her chair started to explain "gold is very expensive to import, if we can get it through customs disguised as dresses we will be quid's in. We will only import a couple of 'special dresses' per month, the rest will be legitimate just cloth dresses. The special dresses will be collected from the shop by our associates in the UK acting as VIP customers"

"That's all very well, but what happens if I am caught with these 'special dresses' in the shop" now I really did feel frightened "it will be alright for you and Don here in the Caribbean, it will be me that's hauled off to jail"

"That's why Don wanted you to stay in total ignorance, if the worst happens and somehow our project is discovered all you would be able to confirm is that you are selling dresses. But with the knowledge that you now have if you are ever questioned it will all rest on how good a liar you are" a half smile formed on her lips "and to be perfectly honest a liar you are not!"

"Oh dear god Suzie, I know when I got divorced that I wanted a bit of excitement but I never thought for a moment that coming here for a holiday would first make me a madam and now an accomplice to gold smuggling" at this point I didn't know whether to laugh or cry.

Before retiring for bed and a much needed sleep, Suzie had told me that we would be travelling to one of her most remote warehouses so that I could see, what she liked to call her project, for myself.

The next day was another extra hot one. I had dressed in a maxi dress and sandals with my hair tied up in a high pony tail. As I walked through the house I could hear Suzie talking to someone on the front porch, their voices sounded quite hostile "I don't know what you think will be gained from this" a man's voice drifted through the open window to the left of the front door.

"If she can see for herself she won't be so scared" they were obviously talking about me "if she thinks that she knows the process all will be good" that phrase from Suzie would circle in my brain in months to come.

I creep back to the kitchen and start clattering cups to make it look as though I have just got up. After a few minutes Suzie comes into the house "I'm afraid there's no time for breakfast we need to get going" turning towards the front door she adds "I'll get Jonathon to stop on route and get us coffee"

The roads leading to the warehouse were narrow and bumpy and not for the first time I am glad that Suzie always travelled in style. Looking out of the window I suddenly thought of Stephen and what he would say about my situation.

"You a CEO of an import company you must be joking. What do you know about business?"

He always conveniently forgot how much I contributed to the company when he first started out, in fact I was surprised that I seemed to know more about planning and cash flow than he did. True he was the engineer who knew all about parts but that alone doesn't make a good company, as our divorce proved. I wonder if she has a good head for business.

Suzie's voice brings me back to the present "We're here" as she gets out of the car she turns to face me "Now Polly, do not ask any of the workers any questions. Store them up and I will tell you everything that you need to know when we leave" her face is set in a stern mask "do you understand" I dutifully nod and we make our way into the warehouse.

Although the building is enormous it is completely shielded from the nearby road by tall trees and thick shrubs, in fact you could drive right by without even knowing that it's there.

The inside of the building is divided into several areas. One has machinists all of which are hunched over their sewing machines, the needles going at break neck speed. There are wooden crates on the floor next to each machinist that seem to be full of dresses waiting to be sewn together. On the other side of the worker are open shelves holding boxes of beads and crystals, each box has a picture on the outside depicting the contents. Beyond the open shelves a woman is meticulously inspecting finished dresses, snipping off stray strands of cotton and then placing them on wooden stands. In this area there are what look like large steaming machines, another worker is carefully steaming the garments whilst a third woman folds and places them in blue boxes.

The second area seems to be a cutting room, bales of different colours of very expensive looking cloth are stacked on shelves that reach from the floor to the ceiling. There are two men at each bench who are using various tools to cut and shape the material that is spread out on their work benches.

The last area is accessed through a heavy steel door, I'm surprised to see that two very muscular guards are positioned in front of the door and only move aside when they recognise Suzie. I again get a feeling of foreboding that sends a shiver down my spine, not for the first time I wonder what the hell I am doing here.

As we walk beyond the heavy steel door we enter a narrow but brightly lit corridor with brick walls running the length of this part of the building. On each side of the corridor a huge glass window is set into the thick brick walls. Through the window on the left hand side, I see 6 figures all dressed from head to toe in white suits, like the ones that you see detectives wearing on TV when they're at a crime scene, each figure is unrecognisable as male or female due to the full face masks they are wearing. Clothes hangers with underskirts are hung on a track that seems to come in from the first area of the building and then makes it way around this room. The white suited individuals are each spraying, what I assume is the liquid gold, onto each garment as it stops in front of them.

Through the window on the right hand side of the corridor I see people, mostly woman, sewing underskirts into dresses. The same scenario is taking place in this area as the first with a woman inspecting each dress and then the steaming process and finally the wrapping. The only difference in this area is that each dress once folded is placed into black boxes. I want to ask Suzie why these woman are also wearing the suits and face masks, but remember that no questions are to be asked within the confines of the building.

As I look through the window at the woman I notice a burly bored looking guard sitting in the corner, he's seems to be playing some sort of game on his phone and is oblivious to anything going on in the room. The look on Suzie's face as she observes him, tells me that she is not at all pleased and I half expect her to barge into the room and give him a good roasting. But she just turns abruptly away from the window and we continue on our tour. It seems strange to me that since entering the building not one person has spoken or looked at us, other than the whirl of machinery the place is dead quiet.

At the end of the corridor is another huge steel door, but to my surprise we do not enter. As we get closer to the door a strange smell hits my nostrils, I know that Suzie has smelt it as well as she quickly turns and marches me back along the corridor and out into the first area.

"Polly I need to deal with something, would you mind waiting in the car for a moment?" as she gently pushes me towards to exit she beckons Jonathon to join her and they both disappear back through the steel door and into the corridor.

After what seems like hours Suzie and Jonathon, along with another man that I have never seen before, walk out into the sunshine. I can tell from Suzie's body language that she is not happy with the man. She keeps gesturing towards the building, as their animated discussion continues the man's whole demeanour changes and by the end he looks totally crushed. After one final wag of her finger at him Suzie turns away and starts walking towards the car with Jonathon close on her heels.

As she climbs in I tentatively ask "Is everything alright?"

"It will be when that bloody fool gets his act together" she nods her head towards the man who is still standing at the doorway to the building "call himself a manager! If he doesn't get his act together and quickly the only thing that he will be is fish food"

Little did I know at the time that this statement would come back to haunt me.

Chapter 13

The next couple of weeks fly by in a whirl of activity, I arrived back in London to find that the work on the shop was well under way. The place looked fantastic, the inside had been designed with black and chrome hanging spaces and down the centre of the first part of the shop was a long black table that would be used to display the accessories that the customers would need to complete their outfits.

The VIP area was exceptionally plush, with big cream sofa's that were covered in huge cushions. In one corner was a small bar with shelves behind that were ready to be stocked with the finest champagne and crystal ware. A small fridge had been installed to the right of the bar and Don informed me that this would always hold the best caviar, he had already placed an order with one of the top stores to ensure that fresh caviar would be delivered at a moment's notice.

The day that I arrived back Don, who had been back in London for the past week, informed me that he had arranged for several girls to come to the shop for interviews. From the way that he was talking about the individual candidates, I suspected that he already knew them through his London associates. Unsurprisingly they all trooped in, one after another on their 6 inch heels. From now on I would refer to these girls as Barbie clones. Plastic pretty with long legs, long hair and big breasts. However, I conceded that pretty girls sell, so I bowed to Don's wish and said that I would give them a fair try.

I had settled into a routine of staying in my new and very swanky penthouse from Monday to Friday and then travelling back to Somerset for the weekend. This seemed to be working fine whilst the shop was still under construction but I was beginning to think that it may not work once the shop was fully up and running. After speaking to all of the Barbie Clones on an individual basis none of them seemed to have any brain cells. I broached this with Don and told him that I needed an assistant manager with a brain, preferably someone slightly older who could be in charge when I was absent.

It was a rainy Monday morning and my taxi had been late picking me up and the traffic was horrendous. After sitting in a bumper to bumper jam for nearly half an hour I decided to get out and walk the final mile. I'd forgotten that I had on 4 inch heels and before long my feet started to complain. As luck would have it I was right outside of a coffee shop and on entering I ordered a flat white and turning to survey the scene noticed that all of the tables were already taken.

However, in the far corner sitting all alone was an older lady. Cautiously weaving my way past prams and discarded umbrella's I approached her "Excuse me do you mind if I join you?" she looked up and nodded "everyone seems to have the same idea today" I took out my phone and starting texting Don telling him that I would be in later.

"Are you late for work" she spoke in a soft accent that I couldn't place

"Just letting them know that I'll be in later" for the first time I looked directly at her, she looked sad and if I wasn't mistaken had been crying "are you alright?"

"Oh yes" looking down into her now nearly empty coffee cup "just another rejection this morning. Everyone wants young people even though they have no experience, employers think that once you're over 50 you should lie down and die" her eyes shot up to meet mine "sorry, sorry just needed to get that out"

"No problem, sometimes it's easier to talk to a stranger" I smiled at her, there was something about her that I liked maybe it was her honesty "what type of jobs have you been looking for?" looking at her sitting there in her shabby coat, which had obviously seen better days, I thought maybe house cleaning or waitressing something along those lines.

"I used to be a department manager in the big Briggs store that closed down last year" she runs her hand down over her coat "although looking at me now you'd never think it!"

"Do you have references?" my heart was in my mouth as I watched her fumble in her bag and bring out several pieces of paper "Do you mind if I look at those?" she handed them over without a word. My eyes flicked over her CV which told me her name was Marie Martinez, 10 'O' Levels, 4 'A' Levels, a letter from her last employer describing her as an exemplary employee of 20 years. All of the time that I had been reading her documents I could feel her eyes on me, finally looking up and without hesitation I stated "Marie, the rain this morning must have been heaven sent"

"I don't understand! Heaven sent!" her eyes were searching my face

"I would like to offer you a job" at that moment I think that we could have both cried "I'm opening a very exclusive dress shop just down the road at the Royal Mall and I need someone with a brain to help me run it"

"Do you mean it? You would employ me even with me looking like this?" her voice was low as if she was fighting to hold back her tears.

"Even looking as you do" I stop and smile at her "but we will have to smarten you up" cringing inside I continue "sorry that sounded very blunt"

"Sound as blunt as you like if there's a job at the end of it I don't mind" she looked past me and out of the window "heaven sent, yes the rain was definitely heaven sent"

After further discussion which resulted in me giving her £200 to get her hair done and to buy a nice black dress I want all of the staff to wear black, this didn't go down too well with the Barbie clones as apparently it doesn't enhance their eye colour or some such nonsense. I leave her with the understanding that she will be at the shop at 10.00 the following morning. Walking out of the coffee shop the rain has stopped and I start wondering what Don will say about me picking up an under manager without his say so, "oh well too bad" I get a funny look from a man passing me, as I must have said that out loud and not, as intended, in my head.

A week or so later during one of our meetings to discuss how the shop would operate with the Barbie clones and who would be responsible for what, Jemma, one of the more together clones tentatively asked "But what's it called? The shop what's the name? We keep calling it 'The Shop' but it has to have a name!"

Don, Marie and I all looked at each other in total silence "You have a very good point there Jemma" Don smiled one of his special smiles at the now beaming girl "How about we have a suggestion from everyone and we" he indicated to the three of us "will chose a winner"

The clones all chimed in with ideas such as "Babes do dresses" "Royal dresses" "Bling is the thing" and so on. In desperation I brought the session to an end as I added "All of these are good ideas" adding in my head 'Not' "but I thought that as all of you and Marie were, in my opinion, heaven sent why not call the shop 'Heaven Sent'" to my surprise everyone thought that this was a great idea and so 'Heaven Sent' was born.

After months of waiting the shop is finally ready to open and a Grand Opening Night has been arranged. Black and Gold invitations had all been hand delivered to the wealthiest families in the area announcing the event and much to our great delight all but one invitation had been accepted.

The Barbie Clones were ecstatic at the thought of putting on a fashion show for the wealthy local ladies and their enormously wealthy husbands. At dead on 9.00 pm, on the night of the event, the guests started to arrive in a line of very shiny limousines each with a livered chauffer, bringing the crème de la crème to our shop door.

The night started off slowly with chit chat between the ladies and the men eyeing up the Barbie clones. These men reminded me of the one's that had attended the yacht party, all were dressed in very expensive tuxedos with diamond cufflinks that glittered under the crystal chandelier. They all exuded power and wealth and I instinctively knew that given half a chance they would rather take one of the Barbie's home with them rather than their older demanding wives.

At exactly 11.00 pm Don switched on the microphone and announced that the fashion show would be commencing in 10 minutes. The gold and satin cushioned chairs that lined either side of the catwalk were soon full and with the help of the fine champagne and caviar everyone seemed to be ready to spend, spend, spend.

It's was gone 2.00 am when the last of the guests left and I hand Marie a glass of bubbly and we drink to a very successful night. Most of the dresses that were shown had been sold and orders for a variety of different colours in the styles had been taken. Earlier when we had quickly totted up the deposits on the orders it came to approximately £100,000 but once the dresses had been made and paid in full the final total would be nearer £300,000, Marie had given a low whistle "I can't believe how much these people are willing to pay for a dress"

The next day the first of the 'special dresses' arrived, the Barbie clones had all been given strict instructions that any dress delivered in a black clothes bag was to be given to either Marie or myself. The only dresses that were to be put in the stock room or displayed would always be in blue bags. Marie never questioned why these were special and it wasn't until much later that I found out why.

It was a few days later when our first VIP customer entered the store, he was well over 6 feet tall and had the physic of a basketball player, his large diamond earring sparkled against his dark skin. The Barbie Clones were almost beside themselves. Marie quickly walked forward and after a short greeting, much to the consternation of the hair flicking Barbie's, whisked him into the discrete VIP area. I joined them and after checking his ID, something that Don had insisted on, he confirmed that he didn't want to look at the dress. He reached into his pocket and handed over a large wad of cash and as this happened I saw a flicker of confusion cross Marie's face but she just handed the black bag containing the dress to him and he was gone.

At the beginning a black bag would arrive every two or three weeks, which resulted in the same exchange transaction. But the deliveries would soon reduce to once a week. On one of my regular calls to Suzie I mentioned that I thought the deliveries were becoming too frequent, but she just laughed and said that it was fine. Little did I know at the time that this conversation would come back to haunt me in the near future.

Chapter 14

Driving out of London towards Somerset not for the first time do I think how lucky I was to stumble across Marie in that coffee shop, she is an absolute treasure. Nothing gets past her, the Barbie clones are now all wearing smart knee length black dresses with minimum make up and actually seem to be learning how to act and sound professional.

The shop has been so busy that we are now thinking of extending the opening times. The ladies who lunch have become regulars and very often buy two or three dresses at a time, much to Don's delight. The only fly in the ointment is the weekly delivery of 'special dresses'.

Before I know it I am turning the car into my driveway, a wave of happiness spreads over me as I so love this place. Swinging my weekend bag out of the boot I almost skip up to the front door, I'm that happy to be home. As I unlock the door I notice that a parcel has been pushed behind the flower pots that stand on the porch floor, turning it over I notice a Barbados post stamp "What the hell" I mutter to myself as I step over the threshold and into the hallway.

I drop my weekend bag on the hall floor and walking through to the kitchen place the parcel on the wooden table. Crossing to the sink I fill the kettle whilst looking out onto the garden, at this time of year it's full of colour with the climbing roses and the majestic rhododendrons all in full bloom. My ritual after the long drive home is to always wander around the garden whilst I enjoy a cup of tea, but today curiosity gets the better of me. I select a kitchen knife and slice open the brown paper wrapping, there inside is a carefully folded parcel secured in a black clothes bag with a note attached:-

Hi Polly

Sorry to do this to you, but Mr Black can only collect his parcel from you in Somerset. Don't be mad! Give him a call and he will immediately collect it.

Love

Suzie

"Oh bloody hell Suzie" I really don't want this man at my home again "this had better be the last time!"

I tap the number into my mobile and as soon as it rings it is picked up, without waiting I hiss down the phone "I have your parcel please come and pick it up NOW!" without giving him a chance to answer I finish the call. Without thinking I screw the note up and throw it into the kitchen bin.

Within half an hour I hear the crunch of car tyres on the driveway, not wanting him to come into the house I grab the parcel and race out to his car. Thrusting the parcel at him and in the sternest voice that I can manage I tell him "Please make other arrangements, I do not want parcels sent to my home" the look on his face was one of complete surprise. Without a word he takes the parcel and slams his car door shut, I give a sigh of relief as he zoomed off out of the driveway "Thank god, now perhaps I can enjoy my days off"

A hammering on the front door startled me from my sleep. Looking at the clock which stood on the bedside table I could see that it was 2.30 am. I jumped as the hammering started again and I could hear various voices shouting. Quickly I got out of bed and hurriedly opened the bedroom window. I was not prepared for what I saw.

"Up there Sarg. Someone at the window" a uniformed policeman was pointing at me.

"What is going on?" I stammered still half a sleep

"Mrs Oakley, please open the door" a man in a dark suit stepped out from the shadow of the house as he spoke.

I almost fell down the stairs in my haste and was trembling both with shock and fright as I unlocked and opened the front door. As soon as the door was open the police officers raced in, some went straight up the stairs whilst others made straight for the downstairs rooms.

Finding my voice I shouted "will someone please tell me what the hell is going on" turning I came face to face with the man in the dark suit "you wake me up at this ungodly hour and without another word I have people all over my house. What do you want?"

Taking my arm he led me into the sitting room "please sit down" looking over my shoulder at a young police woman he continued "I think that Mrs Oakley could do with a cup of tea"

"Cup of tea, more like a bloody brandy!" what was happening to me?

"Mrs Oakley, please try to concentrate. I know that this has come as a shock and I am sorry that we have had to burst into your home at this 'ungodly hour' but we needed to ensure that no-one else was in the house" he stopped as the policewoman brought in a tray with two mugs of tea and a plate of biscuits "I am Detective Mark Wilson. I am part of the drug squad" with that he handed me a mug of tea.

"Drug squad?" now my head was reeling "I don't take or have anything to do with drugs. So why are you here in my home?" I took a sip of the scolding hot tea "Please there must be some terrible mistake"

The policeman that had pointed at the window stepped into the room "Nothing sir, the house is clear"

"Thank you" Mark Wilson looked back at me "you need to get dressed, PC Bennet will accompany you"

"But he's just said that the house is clear, so why do I need to dress?" I looked from the young PC to him "I really don't understand. Please tell me that this is a bad dream"

"Unfortunately you are very much awake. You need to come to the station with me, so I suggest that you dress" he placed his mug back on the tray and nodded at the PC "take Mrs Oakley upstairs. I'm going back to the station" with that he stood up and strolled out of the room.

On arriving at the police station I was led down a long corridor and shown into a windowless room. The police woman pointed to a chair on the far side of a wooden table "please sit there Mrs Oakley" with that she turned to walk out of the room.

"Please wait. I don't understand what is going on" I pleaded with her "why am I here?"

"DS Wilson will be with you shortly" came the gruff reply, with that she walked out and slammed the door behind her.

A sudden wave of nausea came over me as I took in my surroundings. The room contained just the wooden table that I was sitting at along with four chairs, including the one that I was sitting on. The room was really scruffy with a fairly large single light in the centre of the ceiling, which was covered by some kind of cage. In the corner of the room to the right of the door I noticed what looked like a CCTV camera. I shuddered wondering if someone was sitting on the other side of the camera constantly watching me.

At last the door opened and in walked DS Wilson accompanied by another man who introduced himself as DS Brian Hurford. The two detectives took their seats on the opposite side of the table.

"Well is anyone going to tell me what this is all about? You come barging into my home, drag me down to this" at this I waved my hand around the room "leave me sitting in this filthy cold room for ages, for what?....."

I was just getting into my stride when DS Wilson held up his hand "well if you give me a minute……."

"Give you a minute!" I angrily interrupted him "I've already given you 2 hours!"

"As I was about to say" he continued "we understand that you received a parcel yesterday"

"What! All of this is about that parcel" now I really was confused "the parcel wasn't even for me. If you want that parcel why come to my home, why didn't you barge into Mr Black's home and wake him up, instead of me?"

Both men had started to write in their big black note books "Mr Black, you say the parcel was addressed to Mr Black?" Brian Hurford muttered without looking up from his notebook, when I didn't answer he looked straight at me "did you hear me? You said the parcel was addressed to Mr Black, but we know that's a lie" leaning forward and drumming his fingers on the table "we know that the parcel was addressed to you" he sat back in his chair without taking his eyes off of me.

"Well yes it was" my mind was whirling "but the note inside said that I should ring Mr Black to arrange for him to come and collect it"

"So how do you know this Mr Black?" I really didn't like Brian Hurford as he was beginning to rile me "what is your involvement in the delivery of this parcel? How much are you getting paid for these deliveries?"

"Deliveries? Getting paid? What are you talking about?" if this was a bad dream I wanted to wake up now "I received one parcel from my friend Suzie asking me to phone Mr Black. There are no deliveries and no payment. Just one parcel with a dress for his wife" I didn't divulge to them what Mr Black had previously said about not knowing Suzie or the fact that he didn't have a wife "if you don't believe me look in my kitchen bin, I screwed the note up and tossed it in there"

The two men looked at each other, suddenly Mark Wilson got up from the table and walked over to the door "you say it's in the kitchen bin?" I nodded. Opening the door I heard him speak to someone who must have been waiting in the corridor "send someone back to the house, tell them to look for a note in the kitchen bin" with that he closed the door and walked back to join his colleague at the table "this Suzie, who is she?"

"She's just a friend, I've known her for years. She asked me to go out and spend some time with her after my divorce" I shrugged "nothing sinister, she's just a friend"

After a good few hours they finally let me go home. It seemed strange to me that they were only interested in the parcel and had not mentioned anything about the London shop, but as they hadn't mentioned it neither had I.

Chapter 15

As soon as I shut my front door the tears started to flow, not delicate little tears but huge sobs that racked my whole body. I fumbled my way blindly to the staircase and collapsed in a shaking sobbing heap on the bottom stair. The last time I had sat here was when I had phoned Suzie to tell her that I was going to take her up on her offer to join her in Barbados that was a joyful time this was not!

I felt exhausted everything seemed to be floating around me and I couldn't think straight. "I need a shower" I stated out loud "a shower and a decent cup of coffee"

With the warm water rushing over my body the confusion of the previous night seemed to start gelling in my brain talking out loud usually helped me to clear problems "What the hell had that been about! Why were they being so cagy and wouldn't give me any real explanation. Surely if they knew about the delivery to my home, they would also have connected me to the London Shop. Why had there been no mention of that? I couldn't believe that Suzie would send a 'special dress' to my home, please god let her confirm that she wouldn't? None of it made any sense"

After dressing I made up my mind to phone Suzie, I needed her to clarify who Mr Black was and that it was just an ordinary dress, although deep down I knew that it wasn't. Perhaps she could shed some light on how or why the police would raid my house and not the shop. As my hand reached out towards the phone I stopped myself from picking it up, a thought suddenly struck me what if they had bugged my phone "For god sake Polly "I admonished myself "what are you a spy or something?" but a nagging doubt stopped me from using the house phone "a pay as you go is what I need" I clarified to myself "I'll go into town and then I'll phone Suzie on that" satisfied that this was the answer I grabbed my bag and marched purposefully out of the door.

 The morning had been trying to say the least, the spotty young salesman in the phone shop had made me lose my temper by insisting that I really didn't want a pay as you go but needed a contract phone. After hearing raised voices, mostly mine, the manager of the shop had intervened and after what seemed like hours I walked out with the pay as you go and a very sarcastic "Have a nice day" ringing in my ears from the spotty salesman.

 After finally assembling the phone and adding money to the account, which was trickier than I had expected I once again sat on the bottom stair and dialled Suzie's number. After a while her answer phone cut in "Hi, this is Suzie I'm either out getting drunk or getting laid so leave your message and I'll get back to you" This message normally made me smile, but somehow it didn't seem funny today. "Suzie, this is Polly ring me immediately that you pick this up" quickly adding "only ring on this number, do not ring the house phone or my old mobile number. Suzie this is urgent!" with that I clicked the little phone shut.

The phone ringing made me jump "Polly what's so urgent that you can't let this old cougar sleep" she sounded slightly drunk.

"My house being invaded by hundreds of policemen and being dragged off to a cell" this was a slight exaggeration but I wanted to shock her "all over that bloody parcel for Mr bloody Black!"

"POLICE!" she almost shouted down the phone "what did they say? Had Mr Black already collected the parcel? What department were they?" She didn't sound drunk anymore just panicked.

"Yes the bloody police and not just any department but the BLOODY DRUG SQUAD" this last bit I shouted into the receiver "What the hell was in that parcel? Suzie, please tell me it wasn't drugs!"

"No of course not" but her voice didn't sound convincing "Are there any 'special dresses' at the shop?" When I didn't answer immediately "Polly, please focus. Are there any special dresses at the shop?"

"No. Well there wasn't when I left yesterday unless any have been delivered today. Do you want me to check with Marie?"

"No, it's okay Don's in London he can go over and check" she paused and then to my surprise added "Polly, did they take your passport?"

"My passport? No of course not. Why do you ask?" my mind was in such a whirl that nothing made any sense any more.

"Look I'm sure that there's nothing to worry about, but just to be on the safe side I want you to come back here" I could hear her tapping on what I assumed was her laptop "there's a flight at 5.00 am tomorrow morning from Gatwick North Terminal. I'll book the ticket from here and you can collect it at the airport" after a moments silence "Polly, only bring hand luggage. I'll sort out everything you need at this end. Take care lovely" with that she was gone.

As I walk into the airport my usual fears return, I think that every police officer and all of the security staff are watching me. A saying that my mother always used to mutter when my father would do the same thing over and over again, he had dementia, sprang into my head "C'est reparti, or here we go again!"

Walking as steadily and as nonchalantly as I can manage I make my way to the correct desk and calmly ask the heavily made up assistant for my ticket. After a few clicks on her keyboard and after examining my passport she hands both the ticket and passport to me. She confirms that my flight will be boarding in 20 minutes and advises me that I need to go straight to boarding gate 15. Once in the departure lounge I start to relax a little and am surprised when I eventually look at my ticket and see that its first class. My mind sweeps back to the flights that I have taken with Stephen when he would quietly berate the people who turned left whilst we always turned right.

"I suppose that they think that they're something special" he would mutter as he squashed into the cramped seats of economy "don't they realise that most people on the plane could afford to sit up there" at this he would incline his head to the front of the plane "but most of us are more sensible than to waste good money for a bit of space"

I wondered if when she stole my husband if she had grand ideas of shopping sprees and luxury holidays. He might have a successful company but he's still a skinflint or at least he was for the duration of our marriage.

I for one was glad that I had space to relax, taking the headphones out of their little pouch I switched around the various channels until I found some lovely soft music. Once the meal had been served and I had savoured a very good glass of wine I settled down to try to sleep. My mind was still all over the place and I woke with a start. Hearing a noise to my left I looked across into the soft brown eyes of a man "That must have been some dream? I wasn't sure if you were enjoying it or not?" his eyes seemed to dance as he spoke.

Straightening myself up as best I could "Oh dear, I'm sorry if I disturbed you. That glass of wine seems to have gone to my head"

Holding out his hand in my direction he introduced himself "I'm Joe"

Although I really didn't want to be bothered with small talk, I also didn't want to be rude "Hi, I'm Polly"

"Are you holidaying or business?" when I didn't answer he continued "Sorry don't mean to be nosy, it's my job!"

"No, it's okay. I'm visiting a friend" I didn't want to mention Suzie but let him think that it might be a man, as nice as he seemed I didn't want to be bothered by anyone.

"Lucky you, I'm on business" he still didn't mention what his business was and to be honest I wasn't really interested. I was glad when he leaned his head back and shut his eyes. Something about him disturbed me, but I couldn't put my finger on what it was.

As the plane's seat belt light clicked off I stood and reached up to collect my bag from the overhead locker, losing my balance I bumped into Joe who was also pulling luggage from the opposite locker "Sorry" was all that I could say I turned to be met by those amazing eyes.

"Is your friend coming to meet you? I'm hiring a car so if you need a lift anywhere" I noticed that as he spoke he raised an eyebrow.

"I'm not sure but if my friend can't come, I'm sure that someone will have been sent to collect me" as I spoke I realised how grand that must have sounded.

As we left the aircraft I once again had that dreadful sick feeling in the pit of my stomach, swallowing hard I concentrated on walking as steadily as possible down the metal steps towards the ground. Glancing back at the giant aeroplane I wonder what on earth I am walking into. Suddenly I feel a hand on my arm "Steady, watch the step" it was Joe "sorry to grab you, but you looked as though you were miles away" I thanked him and climbed onto the bus.

Sitting there I again looked back at the giant white aeroplane with its union jack flag painted on the tail and wish that it was taking me back to my lovely house in Somerset. At this moment I would give my right arm to be strolling around my beautiful garden with a nice cup of tea. The jerking of the bus as it starts our journey to the airport terminal brings me back to reality and I feel the queasiness that has taken over my stomach start to rise towards my throat. Fumbling in my carryon bag I find a half full bottle of water and quickly take a long drink to try to quell this feeling.

I go through the normal boring formalities as if I'm in a dream and get a feeling of de-ja-vue as I see Jonathon waiting for me in the arrivals terminal. We go through the same routine, as last time, him taking my suitcase and leading me out to the big white SUV. I hear a low whistle from behind and then Joe's voice "Well I didn't know that I was travelling with a celebrity?"

As I go to get into the back seat of the car, I turn and gave Joe the sweetest of smiles before climbing into the waiting vehicle, he returns my smile with a salute before turning away towards the car hire terminal.

On the journey Jonathon informed me that Don had been to the shop and had confirmed that it was all clear. Apparently Suzie had to go over to St Lucia on business and had told Jonathon to take me to her home and that she would see me in the morning. Looking at the clock on the car's dashboard I saw that it was 10.00 am.

I was glad when we eventually reached Suzie's as my muscles were starting to complain, how I wished that Suzie had a bathtub at her home instead of just showers, I would really have liked a nice long soak. Later standing in the shower with the hot water washing over me, a sudden realisation struck me did this now mean that I could never go home!

I had confirmed with Margaret, who stayed at the house for a good portion of the week whilst I was in London, that she could look after the house for the foreseeable future. I hated lying to her, but for whatever reason I didn't want her to know that I had returned to Barbados. It would be good to have someone moving around in the house, if someone was watching then seeing lights go on and off might make them think that it was me.

It was after 9.00 am the following morning when I finally woke, blearily I headed for the kitchen. My stomach was growling as I hadn't eaten since the meal on the plane, I had just opened the fridge door to see what there was to eat when I heard a key in the lock. Silently I prayed "please let it be Suzie"

"Thank god you're here" she flew across the space that separated us and hugged me tightly "I need to know all about it" holding me away from her "you look dreadful, did you manage to sleep?"

"I'm fine just ravenous" I turned back towards the fridge "looks like bacon and eggs. Do you want some?" That morning even the finest caviar wouldn't have tasted any better than that meal of bacon and eggs.

Suzie picks up the coffee percolator that is bubbly away and pours us both a mug of strong coffee "I need to know what happened with the police Polly" she hands me the steaming mug of coffee "was it just the parcel that they were interested in?"

"That's all they asked me about" after eating and taking a huge gulp of my coffee I was starting to feel a little more civilised "not a mention of the shop"

Suzie thought for a moment "Did you notice if anyone followed you from to the airport?"

"I don't think so. But…" hesitating for a moment my mind went back to Joe "no I'm sure that it's nothing"

"What? Did something happen?" Suzie voice sounded quite shrill

"There was this man on the plane, he seemed to be quite interested in why I was coming to Barbados" scratching my head I continued "he kept saying that he was coming here on business but never said what his business was"

"What was his name? Did he give you his name or a card?" now Suzie sounded quite rattled.

"He just said Joe, his name was Joe" Suzie looked uncomfortable "but the strange thing was that we had only spoken half a dozen words and he asked if I wanted a lift somewhere. Thinking about it now, he did seem to be prying" I stopped before adding "or maybe he was just being friendly"

Chapter 16

I had been staying with Suzie for just over a month when all hell seemed to break loose.

"Polly, Polly for Christ sake wake up" blearily I opened my eyes to see Suzie ashen faced sitting on the edge of my bed cradling the house phone in her lap "its Margaret!" with that she pushed the phone into my hand.

"Margaret?" I stifled a yawn and pushed myself up to a sitting positon.

"For god's sake Polly speak to her"

I pressed the speaker button "Margaret, hello is everything alright?" Suzie let out a laugh and muttered something under her breath "Margaret, are you still there?"

"The police have been here this afternoon looking for you" I could hear the tremble in my friends voice "Polly you didn't tell me that you were going to Barbados, why didn't you tell me?" before I could answer she went on "I told them that you were at the shop in London. When they left I rang the shop to tell you that they want to speak to you and it was then that Marie told me that you had gone abroad. What do they want to speak to you about? Do you know?" I could hear how upset she was and I felt awful for lying to her.

"I'm sorry that I didn't tell you. It was all a bit of a rush" I looked over at Suzie who was now pacing up and down in front of the bedroom window "Did they give you a name or a number for me to contact?"

"Yes, he said he was Detective Sergeant Mark Wilson, but he said that you would already have his number? Why would you have his number? Polly what is going on?" her voice now had a frightened edge to it "I don't think that I want to stay here anymore, I don't feel safe. When are you coming back?"

"I'm not sure" again I looked at Suzie for some inspiration but none was given "if you don't want to stay at the house just lock up and go home" I realised as soon as I had said it how hard it must have sounded at the other end of the line so I quickly added "I'm sorry that you have been put through this. I am really grateful for everything that you have done but I don't want you to stay if you feel uncomfortable"

"I will go home for a few days, will you let me know when you're back" her voice sounded hollow as it echoed down the line.

"Yes of course, Margaret please don't worry I'll sort everything out" as soon as I'd spoken she was gone.

I was just about to hand the phone back to Suzie when it rang again. Suzie ran across the room and snatched it out of my hand "Hello……..Yes this is Suzie……. Yes she's here, just a moment" from the look on her face I knew that it was more bad news "Its Marie!"

"Marie, hi" I tried to sound calm, which was difficult with Suzie pacing and muttering at the side of the bed.

Without any pleasantries Marie's voice crackled down the line "The shops been raided!"

"Oh Christ, is everyone alright" I leaned my head back against the pillows to try to stop the room from spinning.

"Bugger, is everyone alright, were there any 'specials' on the premises" Suzie shouted at me "ask her if they found anything?"

"I heard" Marie sounded angry "Tell that ungrateful bitch that no, there was nothing for them to find and yes Polly everyone here is fine, a bit shaken but other than that alright" she paused "thank you for asking"

"What reason did they give for the raid? Did they interview anyone?" my rational brain was starting to work.

"They said that they had information that we had drugs on the premises" her voice now seemed a little calmer "As luck would have it we were just about to close for the day so it was only me and Jemma left in the shop when the police burst in" I heard the sound of a cup being put back on its saucer as she continued "they asked about the dresses and who supplies them. They seemed surprised when we told them that our supplier was in the Caribbean" again the clink of china "They have taken the order book away. I asked them if we can still trade and they have confirmed that we can"

For the second time in less than an hour I found myself apologising "I am so sorry that you and Jemma have been put through this. If you don't feel like opening the shop then don't. Why don't you take a few days off?" I didn't look at Suzie as I added "on full pay of course"

"Thank you Polly, I think that's a good idea. Will we see you soon?"

"I hope so, now go home and have a rest" with that she was gone.

"Fuck, Fuck, Fuck" Suzie was slumped in the chair that stood next to the window "this couldn't have happened at a worse time" she rubbed her hands over her face "Jose arrives today, he is not going to be pleased"

"Jose! Who the hell is Jose?" I spat the words out "Forget about this bloody Jose, shouldn't you be more worried about Margaret and the others who have, through no fault of their own, been put through the wringer!"

"Forget about Jose! Are you bloody kidding? If he's heard about all of this then what they've been through will be nothing to what the rest of us will have to endure" I could tell from her eyes that she was petrified.

I walked over to where she was sitting hunched over in the chair taking her hand I gently stated "I think that you had better tell me who he is and what he has to do with the business?"

With wide frightened eyes she explained "Jose Escobar is the head of the Columbus Cartel, he is arriving today to celebrate our success" at this she gave a sick little laugh "we are supposed to be throwing a party on Tobias's boat tonight" I noticed that she was shaking "bloody hell Polly what are we going to do?"

"Well we could just play it cool and hope that he hasn't heard about it" I stood and stretched my aching legs "Where's Don? Perhaps he'll know how to play it!" a sudden thought struck me "anyway what can this Jose do? How can we possibly be to blame about events in London when we're here?"

Suzie tilted her head to one side as if she was thinking about something before she too had a light bulb moment "You're a bloody genius Polly" Suzie gave a small smile "As you say how can anyone here be held responsible or made to take the blame?"

"Now what's all this about a party, am I supposed to be going to it and if so I hope that you have a decent dress for me" I tried to make my voice sound light whilst my stomach was tying itself in knots, that same old nagging feeling was starting to bubble away in my gut.

Suzie spent the rest of the day either on the phone or pacing the floor which in the end made me feel so uneasy that I tried to cry off of the party "I don't think that I want to attend this party this evening, my head is all over the place and I don't think that I will be very good company"

"Oh no, you have to be there Jose will want to meet you" she walked over to the drinks cabinet and poured two large glasses of rum "he likes to eyeball anyone involved in his business"

"Excuse me, his business? What are you talking about?" I accepted the glass that she was offering to me placing it on the table next to my chair "I thought that this was your business?"

"Well yes it is, but he's my main supplier" she took a slug of her drink "to be honest he's my only supplier"

Later that evening Jonathon pulled up outside of Suzie's in the stretch limousine and as we walked out onto the porch I asked "Are the girls in there?" nodding my head towards the vehicle, when Suzie didn't answer "Oh, no for a moment I thought that it may be a classy dinner as you hold this man in such high regard, but here we go again for another knocking shop night of pleasure"

Suzie grabbed my arm "Don't go on the boat with that sort of attitude, he won't like it" lowering her voice "the girls are coming as a distraction for his boys, he doesn't like them around when he's talking business" with that she walked away and got into the car.

Chapter 17

As I step out of the car onto the dockside my stomach is again doing somersaults as a bad feeling takes over my whole body and I genuinely feel sick. As I stand looking up at the yacht I can hear Suzie, who is still in the car, issuing instructions to the girls. The girls eventually emerge from the car and wiggle their way up the gang plank towards two burly men who have been watching our arrival, they are obviously guarding the entrance to the yacht. As the girls are about to step onto the deck the men say something to them and they immediately raise their arms in the air. One by one the men frisk them and then run a metal detector over each girls body and when they are satisfied the girls are allowed to pass.

Suzie takes my arm as we walk towards the yacht "Remember what I said Polly no attitude" She steps in front of me and as she nears the men she automatically raises her arms, I follow suit.

The girls all head off through the door to the salon and I guess that Jose's men are waiting in there to be entertained, as a loud cheer goes up as the girls make their entrance.

A raspy voice with a very thick accent emanates from our left although I can't be sure, but I would think its owner could be either Mexican or South American. For some reason the sound makes my skin crawl

"At last we meet" I turn in the direction of the voice and to my amazement see a wizened little man who can't be more than 5 feet tall with greasy long dark hair pulled back in to a pony tail that falls half way down his back. I desperately try not to smile at his attire, as he has a white shirt open down to his navel with the biggest medallion draped around his neck. His spindly little legs are encased in tight black trousers and the whole ensemble is finished by a pair of highly decorated boots. His face is the colour and texture of dried leather, but the most striking thing about him is his eyes, they are vibrant green and as narrow as a snakes.

"Turn around" I do as he orders and as I come back to face him a shudder runs through my body "Not bad for an old broad. I take it that Suzie has filled you in and you understand what tonight is all about?"

I'm about to answer when Suzie quickly speaks "its okay Jose, she's completely up to date" she shoots a look in my direction "No problems here!

Now do I spy chilled champagne" She nudges me to start walking "Shall we enjoy a glass before dinner?"

Jose turns on his Cuban heels and with a click of his fingers a man jumps forward and pours the champagne "how many girls have you brought?" as he speaks he licks his lips "I hope that they are good" with that he rubs his hand on the front of his trousers and sneering continues "my boys haven't been home for a long time, so they are looking forward to a very good time" he moves closer to Suzie "they better not be disappointed!" Suzie confirms that her girls are the best and that no-one will be left unsatisfied "Good now where is Don? He should be here"

"I don't know as I haven't spoken to him today" as she speaks she glances at her watch "would you like me to call him?"

"No" I have to try very hard not to cringe as he looks me up and down "it might be better if he's not here, I have some things to discuss with you two lovely ladies and he might get in the way" turning away he waves a hand towards the upper deck and the yachts engines start up.

"I really think that we should wait for Don" I say more to Suzie than anyone else "after all he's very much part of the business" Suzie doesn't answer but I can tell from her eyes that she is now very worried. I know that I would feel a lot safer with Don on board and I get the distinct feeling that so would Suzie.

Before long the dock is a distant blip on the horizon and any hope of Don joining us has quickly disappeared. As we walk through to the dining room Suzie quietly whispers "Whatever happens stay with me" from the way that she squeezes my hand I know that she also feels that this is not a good situation.

As we take our places at the table I notice that a fourth place has been set and I assume that the table was laid in anticipation of Don being on the yacht. Suddenly I notice that Suzie goes very pale and is staring past me to the deck area, as I turn to follow the line of her eyes I see the biggest man that I have ever seen lumbering towards us. He must be at least 6'7 and weigh a breath taking 600lbs. Without a word he joins us at the table and Jose indicates to the male servant to serve the dinner.

The dinner itself is remarkable, lobster tails with caviar and finely cooked vegetables all served on the finest bone china and although it looks and smells delicious I don't have an appetite. Surprisingly most of the conversation is pleasant. Jose asks about my family and I tell him that I really don't have any now that both mum and dad have past. He tuts at this and says that he would be lost without his wife and 10 children. The other man doesn't utter a word but just sits and eats.

At the end of the meal Jose suggests that we all take a brandy and sit outside to enjoy the evening air, once we are all seated he turns to his companion and with a sneer says "Well my friend, why don't you tell these lovely ladies why you have joined us tonight" without moving his head he looked at us from the corner of his eye, for a moment he reminded me again of a snake which was about to strike "I'm sure that they're anxious to know" he leans closer to the other man and mutters "Por favour cuenteles sobre neuestro problema, mi amigo"

The big man leans back further against the cream leather cushions and takes a long drag on his big fat cigar, narrowing his eyes he looks straight at the two of us "I've had some news from London" I feel Suzie tense on the seat next to me "I'm told that there has been some raids, now it puzzles me why neither of you…"stopping to take another drag on his cigar "or come to that Don thought that it was not important enough to mention it to us" Suzie started to speak "Shut up I haven't finished speaking" his voice was unusually high for such a big man "first I'm told that a few weeks ago your house was raided" he pointed his cigar at me "and that you were questioned at the police station and then only yesterday the filth are back at your home again, closely followed by the London shop being raided" his dark eyes seemed to glint in the moonlight "so how much did your friend Margaret know?"

"Margaret?" I couldn't stop the tremble in my voice "Margaret didn't even know that I was out of the country"

"So how did she know to send them to the shop?" Jose leaned forward in his seat as he spoke.

"She thought that I was in London and assumed that as they wanted to talk to me that I would be there" I didn't like the tone of this conversation at all and tried to calm the atmosphere down "I'm sure that all of it is a case of mistaken identity, after all what would the drug squad want with either me or the shop?"

"Is she a bloody idiot or what?" Jose addressed this question to Suzie "what does she mean what would the drug squad want" jumping to his feet he shouted at me "the bloody drugs you moron that's what! You say that she's not an idiot and I say that she bloody well is" with that he slapped me so hard across the face that I went flying across the leather cushions and fell at the big man's feet with a thump.

Shaking my head to try and clear my thoughts I looked up at him from my crumpled position on the deck boards "Drugs? What drugs?" I looked across at Suzie who was now quivering with fear "you didn't tell me about any drugs, you told me gold, liquid gold!" when she didn't answer I pleaded with her "Suzie, you told me gold, please tell them that I know nothing about any drugs"

Both the big man and Jose were now both looking from Suzie to me and back again in total confusion, until suddenly the big man let out a huge belly laugh "Oh, I see you told your friend gold so that she would join you, if you had been told drugs you would have said no, am I right?" with that he prodded me with one of his huge feet, when I didn't answer he gave me a swift kick in the ribs "did you hear me? What sort of idiot are you? Did you really think that we would set up this whole organisation just to smuggle some gold" At this both men laughed "Christ you really are stupid!"

"So are we to believe that neither you or any of your helpers in London have blabbed to the filth" Jose bent down level with my head, I was still winded from the kick in the ribs and found that I could only nod my head in reply "Unfortunately for you, we can't let you go back to London if they're still interested in you" he looked to where the other man was still sitting and menacingly added "can we?" straightening up he ordered me to get to my feet, once I was standing and without taking his eyes off of me he continued "take off your dress" when I didn't do it immediately he took a step towards me "take it off or he will take it off for you" with that he indicated to the other man. My hands were trembling so much that I found it hard to unzip my beautiful dress but at last the zip moved and the dress fell to the ground, Jose looked me up and down and turning to the big man stated "such a nice body, such a waste"

I heard a gasp from Suzie "Jose, please she hasn't said anything to anyone" her eyes were darting wildly between the two men "I can vouch for her, she really did think that it was liquid gold and not coke. I knew if she knew the truth that she would have nothing to do with it. Please Jose, please don't do this!"

In what seemed like one movement he had grabbed Suzie's arm and pulled her to her feet "Someone has to pay for my lost revenue, maybe you'd like to take your friends place "his eyes seemed to bore right into her soul "With your silence I take it that's a no" swinging her round by her arm he growled "Get in there" he pushed her towards the entrance to the Salon "and stay in there until I tell you to come out" Without looking at me she did as she was told, leaving me alone trembling with fear on the deck in just my bra and knickers, not knowing or understanding what these two maniacs had in store for me.

Once Suzie was out of sight Jose, without taking his eyes off of me took my face in his hands and in a soft voice mutter "Cuanto antes esto termine, mejor"

As soon as the words had been spoken the big man slowly got up from his seat, as he stood he threw the rest of his cigar over the side of the yacht and into the sea. Before I could move he had lifted me off of my feet and with my face so close to his that I could smell the cigar smoke on his breath, he swung me up into his arms as he flatly said "Time to feed the fishes" with that he dropped me over the side of the yacht and into the cold dark water below.

Chapter 18

The coldness of the water took my breath away. I felt myself sinking down through the dark water into its murky underworld, the water seemed to be sucking me down and down into its hidden belly as if it was ready to consume me. I honestly thought that I was about to die but my survival instinct suddenly kicked in and I fought my way back up to the surface. As I struggle for breath I see the lights on the yacht as it moved further and further away, even in my panicked state of mind I was sure that at any minute Tobias would swing the yacht around and they would come back and fish me out having taught me a lesson, how wrong was I!

As the hours slipped away my limbs, from numbness brought on by the cold and fatigue from treading water, started to feel heavy and I could feel myself gradually slipping away. Remembering my swimming lessons from years ago I decided to float on my back to give my body a break and started to quietly sing to myself so that I wouldn't fall asleep. I knew that if I slept that it would mean certain death.

The sounds of the sea at night will always haunt me, random splashing noises seem to be magnified in the quiet of the night. Suddenly something big seemed to be diving in and out of the water not far from where I was lying, trying to keep as still as possible I tried to work out exactly where the sound was coming from. A thought suddenly makes me stiff with fear and I send a prayer up to the heavens "please god don't let it be a shark, I don't want to end my life in the belly of a shark" in the back of my mind I am sure that I have read somewhere that it is now very rare to find sharks in the Caribbean, but knowing my luck tonight this would be one of those rare occasions.

My only hope is that once Suzie is safely back on shore that she will alert someone, maybe Don, and I will be rescued. I have to make sure that I get through tonight talking aloud to myself seems to help so I start to not only sing but recite any poems that I can remember, ironically I remember every verse of the 'Old Man of the Sea' a poem that my Grandfather used to tell me. Thinking about it now I realise that it was actually more of a sea shanty than a poem. But floating in the middle of nowhere I guess that it doesn't really matter what it was, reciting it is keeping me awake.

At last the sky begins to get light, I have no idea how long I have been alone floating and drifting in and out of sleep. I look around hoping that I may see land, but all I see is the vast expanse of the ocean.

I don't understand how Suzie could have just left me here however frightened she is, surely she must be able to find a way to get someone to come back and rescue me. Something triggers in my brain and I'm assuming that she made it back to shore, but how do I know that she isn't out there floating in the dark water like me. Frantically I start to scan the surface of the ocean for as far as I can see, but there is nothing, no land, no Suzie and more importantly no boats.

My lips and mouth are so dry that I can literally feel my lips crack when I try to speak out loud. The sun is beginning to rise and I know that before long the temperature will be unbearable, the heat will only make my salt soaked skin dryer and I am terrified that it will crack and bleed, alerting any passing shark to my presence.

I must have slipped into sleep as when I open my eyes the sun is high in the sky and I gauge that it must be around noon. A little voice deep in my brain starts talking to me "why prolong the inevitable, you're going to die so just get it over with. No-one is coming. They all think that your dead anyway, the papers will say 'Middle-aged British woman lost at sea after a night of drunken debauchery on a friends yacht' I imagine who will be at my funeral, Margaret will be distraught and Steve, well he'll most probably celebrate. I don't suppose that Suzie will be there.

Just as I am seriously contemplating diving down into the deep blue sea a noise arouses me from my despair. At first I can't make out what it is but suddenly realisation kicks in, it's a helicopter flying low over the ocean. A sudden surge of energy fills my body and I frantically wave, I don't shout as I know that over the noise of the engine that they won't hear me. To my horror the helicopter flies over me and continues on into the distance. Tears of despair flow down over my salt cracked cheeks, as I watch the helicopter disappear towards the horizon.

"Well that's it" the nagging little voice starts up again "they won't search this area again, it will have been given the all clear. Face it you're on your own"

"God if you want me to die then make it quick" I shout up at the sky above "I'm just going to lie here in this bloody ocean and you can come and do your worst. Just bloody well get on with it"

As the daylight starts to fade I know that I cannot survive another night. I'm starting to see things, today I found myself trying to swim to what I thought was a little island only to look again and it had gone. Dehydration is setting in and I know that I won't last much longer. Scanning the horizon I see a boat which seems to be heading towards me "For Christ sake God do you really have to play these tricks on me, just let me die" I close my eyes and feel myself start to drift into sleep silently I pray that this will be the end.

Suddenly I feel something tugging at my arms and a voice calling my name, for a minute I think that God has answered my prayers and that an angel has come to take me to my eternal resting place. But wait, I hear a number of voices and someone's hands are firmly under my armpits hauling me upwards.

"Polly, Polly can you open your eyes" a male voice sounds very close to my ear. Slowly I open my eyes, but my sight is blurry and I can't make out who it is, the same voice now sounds quite triumphant "She's alive, thank the lord she's alive" As my sight starts to clear I look straight into the worried eyes of Don.

Chapter 19

I awoke with a fright. Looking around the room I couldn't place where I am, it certainly isn't Suzie's. This room was all white and chrome not at all like Suzie's colourful house, this place is far too plain with no colour anywhere. I can't get my bearings. The last thing that I remember was seeing Don, so where is he now? Everything feels really strange, is it me or is the room moving. I can hear what sounds like a distant hum maybe the sound of an engine in the distance.

Lying there I start to panic maybe the movement is the sea and I'm back on the boat. What awful thing do they have planned for me now! Again for the umpteenth time since being thrown into the sea I start to silently pray "Dear God, please don't let me be back on that boat. Please don't let them hurt me again"

As I try to move my body seems to scream out, the pain is unbearable. My skin is so sore and taut from being in the sea for so long, that just trying to move feels like torture. I slowly try to move my arm and as I do I notice a tube that is attached by a needle in my arm. A clear liquid is gently dripping from a bag, which is held high up on a metal stand and I can see the clear liquid running down inside the tube towards the needle in my arm. What if they're trying to poison me, they couldn't drown me so now they're going for a sure fire way to finish me off. Just as I am trying to summon up the strength to remove the needle the door opens and in walks Don "Glad to see that you're awake at last" for some reason the sound of his voice makes me feel safe.

"Where am I?" my voice comes out in a squeak as my throat is so sore and as I try to swallow, tears of pain start running from my eyes, I manage to croak "Don, am I safe?"

Walking across the room he pulls a chair up to the side of the bed and gently taking my hand he quietly says "Yes" he seems to find it difficult to look at me and with his eyes still firmly fixed on the bedsheets he says "Polly, I am so sorry for what has happened to you, we had no idea that they would go so far"

"We! You said we. Do you mean you and Suzie? Where is she?" my questions came out in this strange little voice.

"No, not Suzie and me" at last he raised his eyes to meet mine "Polly, I work or should I say worked undercover for the drug squad, back in the UK" he pauses as if waiting for me to say something and when I don't he continues "for the last couple of years I have been working out here to try to bring down the Columbus Cartel, which as you now know is run by Jose Escobar and Pablo Cortenda. It was their plan to infiltrate the UK's drug market to see if the 'special dresses' would get past customs, if they did then they were planning to take America by storm"

"But what about Suzie?" as I ask I lie my head back against the pillows my eyes feel heavy and I want to sleep "I feel as if I am having a bad dream and that soon I will wake up and none of this will be true. I'm finding it hard to understand. All of this is too much to take in"

On hearing this Don stood "I think that the rest of the explanation should wait until you are feeling stronger"

As he was about to close the door I asked "Don, why does it feel like the room is moving?"

For the first time for a long time I heard that throaty Scottish laugh "The room isn't moving, but the plane is!" at that moment my eyes close and I drift off into sleep.

Something is tugging at me pulling me this way and that "Shark, shark!" I scream as I start to struggle, flailing my arms and kicking my legs.

"Stop, Polly stop" opening my eyes I see a youngish woman standing at my side "I'm sorry but I need to fasten you in we're going to be landing in about 10 minutes" she frowns as she pulls at straps that are crossed over my body "Please lie still"

"Landing? Where are we landing?" I cannot keep the fear out of my voice "Are you taking me back to Barbados?"

"No, of course not" she turns away from me and starts towards the door.

"Please tell me where we are?" I feel very vulnerable strapped into this bed with my head being the only part of me that I can move.

"England!" she snaps the word out "and with any luck straight to prison for you" after checking that no-one is outside the door she struts back across the room and leaning over me with her face only inches from mine she snarls "My brother died from a drugs overdose and if I had my way all of you drug traffickers would rot in jail"

"Well it's a good job that it's not up to you then isn't it PC Noble" a deep Scottish baritone booms from the doorway "Get out. If you know what's good for you you'll keep well away from Polly and me" Don held the door open but as she approached him he stated "As soon as we land report to the airport police do you understand? I don't think that you belong on this case" as she didn't answer he repeated "PC Noble, do you understand?" she curtly nodded her head and disappeared out of the door. "Are you okay?" I confirmed that I was "Good. We will be landing at Gatwick soon, so I need to go and buckle up. I'll see you as soon as we land"

As I lie here strapped in and helpless, the events of the last two days keep swimming around in my head. I still don't understand how anyone could do that to another human being, just throw them in the sea and let them drown. How do these people sleep at night? I thought about Suzie and after all of the years that we have known each other, why would she get me involved in this awful situation. I wondered why Don hadn't mentioned her. Was he hiding something, perhaps she had also been thrown overboard and he didn't want to tell me that she hadn't survived. All of these awful thoughts kept coming and going. I could still smell the cigar smoke on the man's breath, who I now knew was Pablo Cortenda. Nothing seems real, I feel like I'm watching some dreadful Hollywood movie.

"Oh dear god" said that little nagging voice in my head "that awful woman said prison!" lying there I tried to think about any cases of drugs couriers that I had read about in the national press but my mind couldn't focus and as the plane started it's decent the nagging little voice whispered "You'll be old and grey by the time you're free" With that thought ringing in my head I start to weep.

Chapter 20

As the plane touches down Don and another man, who I feel that I should recognise come into the room "You are going to be taken straight to hospital" Don started to release the bed from the floor straps that had been holding it in place "due to the nature of your illness we have told the hospital that you have been involved in a nasty boating accident out in the channel. From now on you will be known as Christina Burton, do you understand?"

"No, not really" I noticed a look that passed between the two men, was it frustration or anger I really couldn't tell.

"Polly! We cannot let anyone know that you are in fact alive. If the cartel know that they were unsuccessful we are sure that they will send someone to finish the job" as Don spoke a shiver shook my whole body "We have secured a private hospital room and our plain clothes officers will act as family members and friends. We are unable to post an armed officer outside the door as this, obviously, would arouse suspicion, but someone will be with you at all times"

As Don and his colleague wheeled me towards the open aeroplane door, I was surprised to see that we were parked away from the terminal in a spot next to a huge warehouse. As soon as we came into sight two paramedics rushed forward and skilfully manhandled me off the bed and onto a stretcher. With a sense of urgency carefully manoeuvred me down the plane's steps and into the waiting ambulance.

Whilst the paramedics gave me a quick health check and secured the bag containing the clear liquid up to a hook that was situated near the roof of the ambulance, I could hear Don and the other man talking in low voices. I was very relieved when Don climbed into the back of the vehicle and travelled with me to the hospital.

The journey took about an hour and by the time we reached our destination I had got used to be called Christina. Don had peppered his conversation with the name so many times that I now answered to it without hesitation. As soon as the ambulance arrived I was whisked straight up to the private wing and into my room.

Don had stopped at the reception desk to speak with the on duty sister asking her to issue instructions to her staff that I was not to be unnecessarily disturbed. He informed her that a family member would be staying with me at all times and would be able to take care of all of my needs. From the little bit of the conversation that I could hear I don't think that the sister was very happy about it and I heard her say "Well I think that we had better see what Matron has to say about all of this" To which I heard Don curtly reply "Tell Matron to speak to Mr Zehan, who as I am sure that you know is an esteemed consultant. I'm sure that he will want Mrs Burton's, who is a private patient of his, wishes complied with. He will confirm that she is to be given the utmost respect and privacy"

As he walks into the room he mutters as he closes the door "Bloody jobsworth"

The following day raised voices could be heard just outside my hospital room door. "Well this is all very strange" a woman's indignant voice could be heard "I've never heard anything like it, after all this is still my ward"

"As I have already explained to you my patient is very fragile from her dreadful experience and I do not want any further stress put on her by all and sundry traipsing in and out of her room." This second voice belonged to a man and from his tone I could tell that he was beginning to get agitated about the whole situation "I believe that this is actually a private wing and as such if I wish for only my private staff to nurse my patient then that is the way it will be!"

"But as Matron I still think…………."

"But as the patients consultant I really do not like to pull rank on you Matron. Should I hear that anyone without my direct permission has entered this room…" his voice now held a hint of aggression "heads will roll. Now if you will excuse me I wish to speak with my patient."

I wasn't sure what to expect as the door opened and was very pleasantly surprised, when a small, very round man with a beaming smile walked into the room. Crossing quickly to the bed, he takes my hand in his and scrutinises my face. In the gentlest of tones he remarks "My dear girl, how on earth have you survived the last few days, only you and god will truly know." After examining my wounds he explains that he will instruct the assigned medical team on the correct way to treat my injuries both physically and mentally.

I have now been in hospital for a week and I am feeling much better. My 'family' members have strangely consisted of, a nurse who every day has been tending to the sores and sunburn on my body. Another 'niece' is a very accomplished hairdresser and has coloured my once mousy hair to a deep auburn. The third 'niece' has brought me new clothes, as the only thing that I had on when they rescued me was my knickers and bra, both of which had quickly been removed and kept as evidence being replaced by a not very complimentary white jumpsuit. My 'nephews' have brought me books and food and have kept me entertained with board games and one has taught me how to play poker. It would have been lovely if I had met all of these people under different circumstances.

On the second Monday of my hospital stay Don walks into the room, one glance at his face told me that he wasn't very happy "Time to go Christina"

A feeling of dread starts to creep through my body "Go! Go where?" I look up at him from my seat next to the window "are you taking me to prison?"

Slowly he walks around the bed and perching on the edge he takes my hand in his "Not exactly" he keeps his eyes on the ground.

"Don! Look at me! Where are you taking me?" I pull my hand away from him so quickly that he is forced to look at me as I repeat "Where are you taking me?"

"We need to move you to a safe house. You can't stay here any longer, people are starting to get suspicious" he nods his head towards the door "that nosy bloody sister has been making comments about how funny it is that there has been no mention of a boating accident on the news." Standing he straightens his tie. "So it's been decided that for your own safety we are moving you to another location"

One of my 'nieces' is already waiting outside of the hospital room with a wheelchair. As soon as we walk out into the corridor I am told to sit in the chair and a thick heavy blanket is wrapped around me. When we reach the ground floor I am rushed into a waiting car and whisked away from the hospital grounds.

As we drive through London I watch the people rushing here and there without what seems to be a care in the world. I think back to how happy I was pottering around the garden and enjoying the odd visit to the theatre which all seems like a life time away. My eyes wander back to the unfolding scene outside and I wish with all of my heart that I was back in Somerset in my beloved garden.

The car suddenly takes a sharp right and I notice that we are heading out of London towards the Midlands. The journey seems to take forever and as the light begins to fade the lights of the cars coming towards us seem to be hypnotic and my eyes start to close.

I wake to Don calling me "Christina, wake up" as I open my eyes he climbs out of the car "here we are home sweet home"

The house itself is nice, but it certainly isn't home! The perimeter is guarded by a row of very tall thick bushes and the little garden has not been loved for a long time. The inside of the house is clean but old with creaking floorboards and windows that rattle in the wind. Still if it's safe then I suppose that's all that counts.

"I thought a nice supper of fish and chips washed down with a decent red" Don hands Tom, the driver, some money "I saw what looked like a decent chippy just down the road, can you pop back and get us all some" as Tom went to leave the room, Don added "and don't forget the red" the younger man made a salute. After we heard the front door close Don looked at me "Are you really alright?"

"Well, now you mention it there are some things that I would like to know" I sat down opposite him at the big wooden table "For instance, where is Suzie? Do you know what happened to her?"

After a moment he flatly stated "She's in jail! All of them are in jail" he tapped his fingers on the table top "When they arrived back in port, we were waiting for them. It's a very rare event that both Jose and Pablo are ever seen together, so along with our Caribbean counterparts we set up a sting to catch them before they had a chance to disappear again"

"Suzie, did Suzie tell you where to find me?" I couldn't look at him.

"I'm sorry to say, that she didn't. In fact as we rounded everyone up and asked if there was anyone else on the yacht it was Honey who asked where you were" he let out a long sigh "if it hadn't been for her we wouldn't have known that you had even been on the boat that evening"

I was speechless as I couldn't believe that Suzie would have just abandoned me, when she had the opportunity to tell someone where I was. After a while I managed to compose myself "what's happened to the girls? Are they also in jail?"

Don shook his head "No, they did nothing wrong. After being questioned they were allowed to go" looking across the table at me he continued "it's strange but whatever you think about the girls lifestyles, Honey was the one that was most worried about you" he reached into his pocket and took out a silver chain with a charm of a small silver spider on it which he handed to me "Talking about Honey I had forgotten she gave this to me and asked that if we found you would I give it to you"

My emotions took over and I was unable to stop my tears from flowing "I remember seeing her wear this" opening the catch I secured it around my neck, my fingers gently caressed the little spider.

"In the Caribbean it's supposed to bring you luck if you see a white spider, I think that's why most of the spider charms are in silver" Don informed me "If I remember rightly it's called 'Anansi' in old folklore"

I started to laugh just a gentle chuckle that quickly escalated into a near hysteric full blown gut wrenching howl. The more I looked at Don's startled face the harder I laughed. It felt so good to at last rid myself of my pent up emotions. The little spider danced at my throat with every roar that left my mouth.

Don quickly got up and raced around the table to where I was sitting, cradling me in his arms he gently stroked my hair as he promised "Once you are feeling better I will explain everything to you, but I don't think that now is a good time" I felt like a child in his arms "Take a couple of days to settle in here and then I promise we will talk" As if on cue we heard Tom's key being pushed into the front door lock "Go and wash your face, once you've had something to eat and a good night's sleep you'll feel a lot better" gently he pulled me to my feet and I did as I was told.

Chapter 21

Over the next few days I settled into the new house, the creaks and groans of the old floorboards became a familiar sound and no longer a scary noise. As the weather was fine, I felt that I was going stir crazy staying in the house all day, so I decided to try and tidy the garden up.

The old garden shed, which stood at the end of the garden, held a treasure trove of old tools and after rummaging around I managed to find everything that I needed. I was so engrossed in trimming and dead heading the various rose bushes that I didn't hear Don approaching, his booming voice startled me so much that I almost fell into the neatly trimmed rose bed "Christina, what are you doing?" he sounded angry "I've told you not to come out on your own! What would you have done if I had wanted to hurt you?" with that he hauled me to my feet "you must listen to what you are told?"

Suddenly I felt really angry and snatching my arm away from him hissed "I am not a bloody child! Do not shout at me!" throwing the secateurs on to the ground in an act of defiance I continued "if I am to be a prisoner and have to stay in at all times then I wish I had died in the sea, at least my soul would be free"

It was as if I had smacked Don in his face he looked totally shocked by my outburst "Please don't say that, I'm sorry for shouting it's just that when I saw that the house was empty I thought............." His voice trailed away as he swallowed hard "Anyway there are things that we need to discuss, so if you don't mind would you come back indoors" with that he turned and briskly walked towards the open back door.

Like a petulant child I slowly followed him back into the house, once inside I made myself comfortable on the big squashy sofa that stood in the middle of the sitting room and listened as he bustled around in the kitchen making coffee. Once he was seated he looked at me and I could see that something was troubling him "What is it? Has something happened to Suzie?"

"No, no" he handed me my coffee "As you know we need the cartel to think that you did indeed die at sea and we have to make the situation as believable as possible" he stopped and I could see that he was trying to decide how to word his next statement "your house in Somerset needs to be sold and Margaret needs to think that you are in fact dead!"

I thought that my heart was going to stop "No" I realised that I had shouted this, so lowering my voice "please Don, there must be another way. I love that house. Why do you have to lie to Margaret? I can't bear the thought of her going through the pain of grieving for me when I'm still alive"

Moving to sit next to me, he takes my hand in his "I'm sorry, truly I am but there is no other way. We have to do everything that would normally be undertaken on someone's death" he looked down at his knees and added "if the cartel gets wind that you are still alive we don't know what they will do. Margaret is the person that is closest to you and our intelligence officers are concerned that if the cartel gets suspicious they may kidnap Margaret to try to flush you out of hiding." A sudden sob that escapes from my lips brings his eyes back up to my face "You have to realise that these people will stop at nothing to get Jose and Pablo out of prison. I'm sorry but you have to understand that to all intents and purposes Polly Oakley is dead and you are now and forever will be Christina Burton"

The next few days were surreal as Don had informed my local police station in Somerset, that I had been killed in a dreadful boating incident in the Caribbean and due to the fact that the boat had unfortunately blown up that there would be no body to bring home. He had asked that one of their more sympathetic detectives should be sent to break the news to Margaret.

Once she had been told, Don sent one of my 'nieces' accompanied by a 'nephew' down to Somerset to meet Margaret at the house. They told her that they were solicitors acting in connection with my instructions in my Will, they asked if she would like any of my personal belongings. They lead her to believe that the proceeds of the furniture and house sale, along with my personal wealth, had been left to charity, so stated that if there was anything that she wanted that she needed to take it immediately. I was not allowed to keep anything not even my mother's jewellery or my father's pocket watch, so I was very glad when I heard that Margaret had asked for these items. It was arranged that a house clearance company removed all of the furniture and the house was put on the market.

The very next week Don received news from 'the solicitors' that a very substantial cash offer had been received for my beautiful Somerset home and that the sale procedure would now start. We were sitting at the big wooden dining table when Don broke this news to me "But what am I to do? I can't stay hidden away forever" I suddenly felt bereft "my life cannot consist of hiding and being afraid all of the time"

"The cartel will only keep looking if there is a chance that you are still alive" for the first time he was unable to look me in the eye, something seemed to be bothering him.

"Don, what is it? There's something that you're not telling me!" looking at his face, deep down I knew that whatever the problem was it must be big "Tell me!"

Keeping his eyes firmly fixed on the wooden table top he started to speak "We have intelligence that two suspected members of the cartel are about to enter the country, they are in fact in transit as we speak. Due to this I cannot be seen here".

Shaking my head I started to plead with him "But you can't leave me on my own. Why can't you stay? Don, please I don't understand?"

"The cartel still think of me as part of the team, remember I supplied men for the 'yacht parties' and was heavily involved with setting up the London shop. Our intelligence think that once the two men arrive that they will try to make contact with me" I could tell from his expression that he was very troubled "if they don't believe me when I tell them that all I have heard is that you died in mysterious circumstances then they might decide to follow me. We can't chance that happening"

"Don, will this ever be over?" I tried to sound calm but my voice gave me away and as I spoke the trembling spread from my voice throughout my whole body "I don't want to be here on my own!"

At last he looked at me "Do you remember when you last flew into Barbados, there was a man who engaged you in conversation?" After everything that had happened over the last few months that man had become irrelevant to me but I did remember him "Well he is one of my finest officers and he will be coming down, in fact he should be arriving at any time to stay with you" Don looked at his watch and frowned "in fact he's late, I need to get going soon, as I must be back in London before the plane lands".

As if on cue we heard the crunch of gravel which heralded the arrival of a vehicle. Don jumped up and standing to one side of the kitchen window peeped out through the blinds in the direction of the driveway. Once he was satisfied that it was the person he was waiting for he made his way to the front door. I heard the murmur of voices, but was unable to hear what they were saying.

Chapter 22

Over the next couple of days Joe and I settled into a routine, he would go out early for a jog and then on his way home call into the little shop at the bottom of the road and bring back an armful of daily papers. We would then scour each one for any mention of the impending drug trial. Day after day there was nothing until suddenly "Oh dear god" was all I could say as I stared at a picture of Suzie looking wild eyed and frightened. She was in what looked like a courtroom and was seated between two very burly female prison officers. The headline seemed to jump off the page at me 'Middle Aged British Woman Held in Drugs Bust' I couldn't bear to look at her face any longer and pushed the paper across the table to Joe.

Silently he started to read the article, but after a while he looked up and said "I think that you should hear this" with that he started to read..........

It is stated by the Barbados authorities that Suzie Gilbert a middle aged woman from Dorset, who immigrated to Barbados a number of years ago, is one of the main ringleaders in a major organisation that has been trafficking drugs into the UK. She along with her associates Jose Escobar and Pablo Cortenda have been, for the last year, smuggling cocaine into Britain under the disguise of dresses that have been sold via a London Shop.

The London arm of the organisation is believed to have been set up and run by Ms Gilbert's long-time friend Mrs Polly Oakley. However, it has been stated in court by the defendant that Mrs Oakley either fell or was pushed over board during one of the infamous yacht parties. Her body has never been found.

Ms Gilbert is also being accused of running a prostitution ring, supplying young girls for wealthy men at the aforementioned parties.

The case against the three defendants continues.

"Joe, do you think that this means that I am safe? I mean if they are acknowledging in court that I'm dead, will they still be looking for me?" I try to read his face for a reaction, when a sudden thought strikes me "Oh God, will I be put on trial here? They said that I am the London arm of this, so will I be held responsible?" I honestly think at that moment that I must be going crazy.

To my surprise Joe starts to laugh "How can you be held responsible if you're dead!" leaning forward he puts his hands flat on the table top "I understand what you mean, but there is no possibility of you going to prison.

You were coerced by us to join the organisation, you were unaware of why it was important for you to be involved. We needed someone who was totally oblivious to what Suzie and her associates were up to. When you turned up out of the blue in Barbados a total innocent, the plan came together"

"So are you telling me that all of my time spent in Barbados and with Don has been a sham?" for some reason I felt totally let down by Don, had he just been play acting all of the time, making out that he liked me just so that he could bring Suzie down.

"We made sure that someone was close by at all times, looking out for you" he didn't seem to want to look at me and swallowing hard he added "although that last night……."

"Yes, what about that last night! I get thrown into the sea and left to die so where was this person who should have been close to me, watching out for me" I knew that it wasn't Joe's fault but he was the only one here "so come on what happened on the last bloody night, that left me thinking that I was going to die in that bloody ocean"

"Our intelligence was told that it was only Suzie going to meet with Jose and Pablo, there was no mention of you" he at last looked at me "When Honey asked where you were I thought that Don was going to go crazy. I've never in all of the years that I've worked with him seen him like that" drumming his fingers on the table he went on "When Suzie was asked where you were and she just pointed out to sea, I honestly thought that he was going to hit her. At first light he sent up the police helicopter and organised boats to search for you" looking down he hesitated "I'm so sorry to tell you, but Suzie sent us in the wrong direction. It wasn't until we spoke to the girls again that Chantelle mentioned that the yacht was heading for St Lucia it was only then that we realised that the search was taking place miles from where you had been left"

I couldn't stop the tears from flowing "Why would she do that?" I stuttered between sobs "We've known each other for years. I held her when her parents passed away and have always been such a good friend. Why would she want me dead?"

"She has been travelling in a different world from yours for a number of years, when you mix with that type of person you have to become hard" he spoke in a soft voice "sometimes they get so caught up in all of it, that somehow none of it seems real anymore. It's as though they are watching a movie and can just turn it off and carry on as normal" He stood and walked over to the drinks cabinet and collected two glasses and a bottle of brandy "it might be a bit early for this but I think that you need it" without turning to face me he pushed a glass of the amber liquid in my direction and continued to speak "The friend you knew in England has been swallowed up by greed of both money and status" when I didn't make any comment he added "Christina, think about this, can you remember how much you were paid for just being a chaperone at the first yacht party? If I remember rightly Don said it was about $5000" I nodded to confirm this "From working those girls alone Suzie would have become a millionaire. The problem is money breeds greed for more money and that's how she got tangled up with the cartel. If she had just stayed as a 'madam' she would, most probably, still be free instead of facing a possible life sentence"

"Bloody hell, LIFE!" I hadn't considered until now how long she would get.

"Christina, you must prepare to hear the worst. If the Barbados criminal court system feels that Suzie had any part in you 'falling' over board....." he stopped and looked straight into my eyes "it could mean the death sentence!"

At that moment I felt as though the room was moving and I gripped the edge of the heavy table to try to steady myself "I suppose that's what they did to me when they left me there............" big fat tears were now rolling down my face and landing with a plop on the table "as fish food!"

Chapter 23

Later that week Joe received a call from London saying that he was needed back in the city for a few days and that a female police officer would be coming down to stay with me. For some reason I felt really uneasy "Joe, was that Don?"

"No, it was dispatch calling on his behalf" as he spoke he continued to gather the few things that he would need to take with him.

"But Joe, Don said that it would always be him that called if our instructions needed to be changed" my stomach was starting to do somersaults "do you think that you should call him, just to check?"

"I really think that you are becoming paranoid. How would they have got my number, Don's the only one that has it" he clicked the locks shut on his case "don't worry"

But I did worry. Something just didn't feel right. Don had specifically said that I would always have one of his best male officers with me. I know that it's not politically correct, but he felt that should the cartel show up that a male officer would be better equipped to deal with the situation. Something very definitely did not feel right.

About an hour later a small dark car pulled into the driveway. Joe gave me a hug and told me not to worry, with that he strolled out of the front door towards the young woman who was getting out of her car. For a few brief moments they talked and then on a shake of hands Joe got into his car and he was gone.

Peering out from behind the kitchen blinds I felt that there was something familiar about this young woman, but I couldn't think why. She had taken a suitcase out of the car boot and was now pulling it across the gravel driveway towards the house. On entering I was surprised that she didn't bother to call out but walked straight through to the kitchen area.

On closer inspection I saw that she was of medium height and build. Her hair was cut in a very sever bob and had been dyed raven black, the colour made her already pale skin look ghostly white. It seemed odd to me that Don would send such a petite officer as protection, especially as he had information that members of the cartel were in England. I pushed these thoughts to the back of my mind. I concentrated on the fact that Joe must have been satisfied otherwise he wouldn't have left me alone here with her.

"Do I hear the kettle boiling?" she had a soft northern accent and again I was sure that I had heard that voice somewhere in the past.

"Are you hungry?" I politely asked

"Bacon butty, would be good" I noticed that she didn't say please and this rankled me a little "which room is mine?" but before I could answer she had walked back out of the kitchen and was heading for the staircase "don't worry I'll find it" she shouted back over her shoulder.

This dreadful uneasiness was starting to creep from my stomach all over my body and I tried to rack my brains where and when I had met this girl before, but try as I might nothing sprung to mind.

The rest of the evening was spent, for the most part, in silence. I had tried to make conversation with her over supper but she made it quite obvious that she wasn't interested in small talk.

Just after 10.00 pm the girl, now known as Emma, locked all of the downstairs windows and doors. To my surprise she put the keys in her trouser pocket, when she saw that I was watching her she said "I'll look after these, we don't want any intruders do we?"

In the early hours of the next morning a sudden noise coming from the kitchen, which was immediately below my bedroom, woke me. I wasn't sure what to do and for a few moments lay there quietly listening to the sounds of movements that could be clearly heard through the old floorboards. Silently I got out of bed and crept out of my room making my way, as quietly as the floorboards would let me, to Emma's room. On reaching her room I hesitated should I gently knock or just walk in! As I reached out towards the door handle a hand clamped down over my mouth and my head was violently jerked back into someone's body.

"Well Mrs Nosy what are you doing creeping around at this time of the morning" the hand seemed to tighten across my mouth as the person spoke "now that you're up you can have your surprise early" the sleep suddenly cleared from my brain as I recognised Emma's voice "I'm going to take my hand away from your mouth, but as you already know it's not a bit of good screaming because there's no-one here to help you" As she spoke she pushed me towards the staircase "get down there"

On entering the kitchen I couldn't believe my eyes, on the table she had laid out syringes, a couple of spoons and some little bags of white powder "Welcome to your house of fun!" she forcefully pushed me towards a chair that had been placed in the middle of the kitchen floor.

As I was slammed onto the big wooden chair I finally came face to face with her, a shudder coursed through my body. A mass of mousy coloured curls had taken the place of the black hair that she had arrived with, her hair now reminded me of my own, before it had been dyed auburn.

I now knew where I had seen her before "You're the one from the plane" she didn't reply but just stood staring at me "but Don said that you were to have nothing to do with me" a light bulb seemed to click on in my brain "the phone call…………….." before I could finish she struck me hard across the face. As I reeled from the shock she started to roughly tie me to the chair with a thick coarse rope that had been stored under the kitchen table.

"Shut up, you stupid cow" her voice was pure evil, it reminded me of the one's that you hear on the detective programmes on the TV when the murderer is caught "if Joe is so stupid not to check, who's fault is that " she turned and started to do something with the items on the table.

"If you're going to kill me, you could at least tell me why" I tried not to sound frightened even though I knew that my end was most probably close.

Turning to face me she hissed "Kill you! You're a good few hours away from meeting your maker, we're going to have some fun first" with that she picked up one of the packets of white powder "but I will tell you why you are going to die. You see this?" she shook the packet in my face "this is what you and your friends killed my brother with"

"I haven't killed anyone" I tried to plead with her "I don't even know what that is"

"I don't even know what that is" she mimicked me in a silly whiny voice "this you stupid fucking woman is Cocaine, Coke, Blow, Big C, Snow or any other fucking name you want to call it" I noticed that as she spoke she balled her fist around the bag of powder and for a moment I thought that she was about to hit me again "this is what killed Harry and this is what will kill you….." she paused and with a stupid smirk on her face spat out the last word "EVENTUALLY." She seemed to be contemplating her next move "killing people is exhausting work, so I think a really good breakfast is called for before I start. " Was my mind already playing tricks on me, was she really going to have breakfast!

As I sat tied to that chair, everything seemed surreal, sitting there watching her whilst she bustled about the kitchen cooking bacon and eggs and making coffee, to an outsider the situation would seem ridiculous like something from a bad horror movie.

As she sat down at the table to enjoy her meal, my mind started to work through the events of the previous day. Surely if Don had not called Joe back to London someone would soon arrive to save me. However, I worked out that he wouldn't have got back to the city in time to meet with Don yesterday as it would have been after 8.00 pm. I'm sure that as soon as he walks into the office this morning all hell will break loose.

Arching my back I try to see the time on the kitchen clock, but it's just out of view. Looking out of the window I can see that the sun is coming up, it's still far too early for them to have realised what has happened. I know that there is no way that she will hold off from hurting me for at least the next 3 hours. I have to try to think of a way to stall her, at least to give them time to try and get here to save me.

The scrapping of chair legs on the stone kitchen floor brings me back to reality. What can I do to stop this insanity? Perhaps if I can get her to think about the consequences of her actions, she might come to her senses.

My voice as I start to speak seems to startle her "I know that you are going to kill me, but have you thought about what will happen to you?" Again she just stares at me. "Have you thought how this will affect your family?" I push on "after all your parents have already lost their son."

"Shut your filthy mouth" before I know what is happening she has leapt across the kitchen and is standing in front of me, her breakfast knife still firmly held in her hand "don't you dare talk about my family with your filthy mouth!" with that she slashes the knife across my cheek, drawing back from me she muttered "next time it will be your throat"

The pain of the knife cutting through my flesh made me reel with shock, I could feel the blood trickling down my face and onto my neck to be soaked up by my dressing gown collar. As she drew her arm back as if to slash me for a second time with the knife, something suddenly makes her stop. Cocking her head to one side she seemed to be listening intently, without a word she swiftly moves across the room to the window overlooking the back garden. Positioning herself to one side of the large window and making sure that she was hidden by the heavy curtain she peers out as if waiting for something to happen.

A sudden noise from the side of the house makes her spring into action, reaching under her jumper she pulls out a small gun from the waistband of her jeans. Quickly she moves towards the side door that leads out into the garden. From my position I can just see the back of her as she crouches down and silently opens the door.

For a moment everything is quiet until a distant noise breaks through the hushed morning air. Straining my ears to make out the sound I realise that the noise is the sound of a helicopter and I start to pray that it is Don coming to rescue me.

My prayers are stopped by a man's voice shouting just outside the kitchen window "Traidor debes morir como un perro" this is followed by rapid gun fire. After that everything goes very quiet.

Sitting tied to the chair I know that if the man comes inside the house, that I won't stand a chance. I start to try to untie the huge knot in the rope but it is impossible, the circulation in my hands has been cut off for too long and my fingers just won't work.

The familiar sound of tyres on the gravel driveway makes me ridged with fear. I can hear the sound of heavy boots running towards the house and the front door being kicked in, the voices in the hallway are getting nearer please god let them kill me quickly. I close my eyes and await my fate.

Chapter 24

Later Don told me that Emma had died from a single gunshot on her way to the hospital. A note had been stuffed into her mouth which read 'Traidor, debes morir como un perro'. One of Don's intelligence officers had roughly translated this as 'Traitor, you must die like a dog', the officer confirmed that this was the Columbus Cartels motto. I told Don that I had heard this being shouted immediately before the shots had been fired.

My heart broke for Emma's parents and I wondered, and still often do, how they coped with the news that their child had been shot in such an awful way. Don tried to reassure me that they would have been given a completely different scenario regarding her death, as it couldn't be revealed that it was a police officer shot dead and not me.

The intelligence office had informed Don that they believe the two members of the cartel had followed Emma, after seeing her leave headquarters with a suitcase, in the hope that she either had information about my death or knew if I was still alive where I was being hidden.

When she walked out of the house on the fateful morning, they must have believed that it was me. Any photo that they would have been shown would have been of a lady with curly mousy hair, very different from the way that they would have seen Emma who had arrived with a short dark bob.

Don pointed out that the only good thing that had come out of the situation was that the cartel would now be convinced that I was dead.

It was two years later when news reached us that Suzie's trial was finally over. All three, Suzie, Jose and Pablo had been sentenced to life imprisonment without the possibility of parole, for their part in the setting up and smuggling of cocaine. Other lesser members of the organisation were given sentences ranging from three to ten years.

Suzie was also charged with being a 'Madam' encouraging girls into prostitution and supplying them for the men at the yacht parties.

No-one was ever charged with my murder.

ABOUT THE AUTHOR

Paula has lived in the West Country for most of her life and now lives in Somerset with her husband of 40 years. They have two grown up sons and five wonderful granddaughters. She retired 6 years ago, after working within the financial sector for over 20 years and now loves nothing better than spending a day at her computer. When she's not writing she enjoys going to the gym, visiting the theatre and most of all spending time with her family.

If you enjoyed reading *Without You,* please consider leaving a review:

- www.amazon.co.uk
- www.amazon.com
- www.goodreads.com

For any further information or to contact Paula online:

- Website: www.paulawilkesauthor.com
- Twitter: Wilkes4paula

Printed in Poland
by Amazon Fulfillment
Poland Sp. z o.o., Wrocław